This book is a fictionalized account of the author's real-life experiences and observations. The lessons he relates are told from the vantage point of Jonah, a long-time commuter on the Metro-North train from Greenwich, Connecticut to the world of finance in New York City. Encounters and reflections have been condensed into a two week time frame to facilitate the story's narrative.

The thread tying the story together is Jonah's search for connections between the nine beatitudes (from Jesus' Sermon on the Mount) and the nine fruit of the Spirit (love, joy, peace, patience, kindness, goodness, faithfulness, gentleness, self control; Galatians 5:22-23). Along the way, Paul, a wise and mysterious train conductor, answers Jonah's questions and guides his thinking.

This book was written in part to encourage readers to be aware of their own stories, how they evolve over time, and the importance of building character based on Christian values.

The Early Train
Signs Along the Way

Winged Lion Press
Hamden, CT

ISBN 13 978-1-935688-31-0

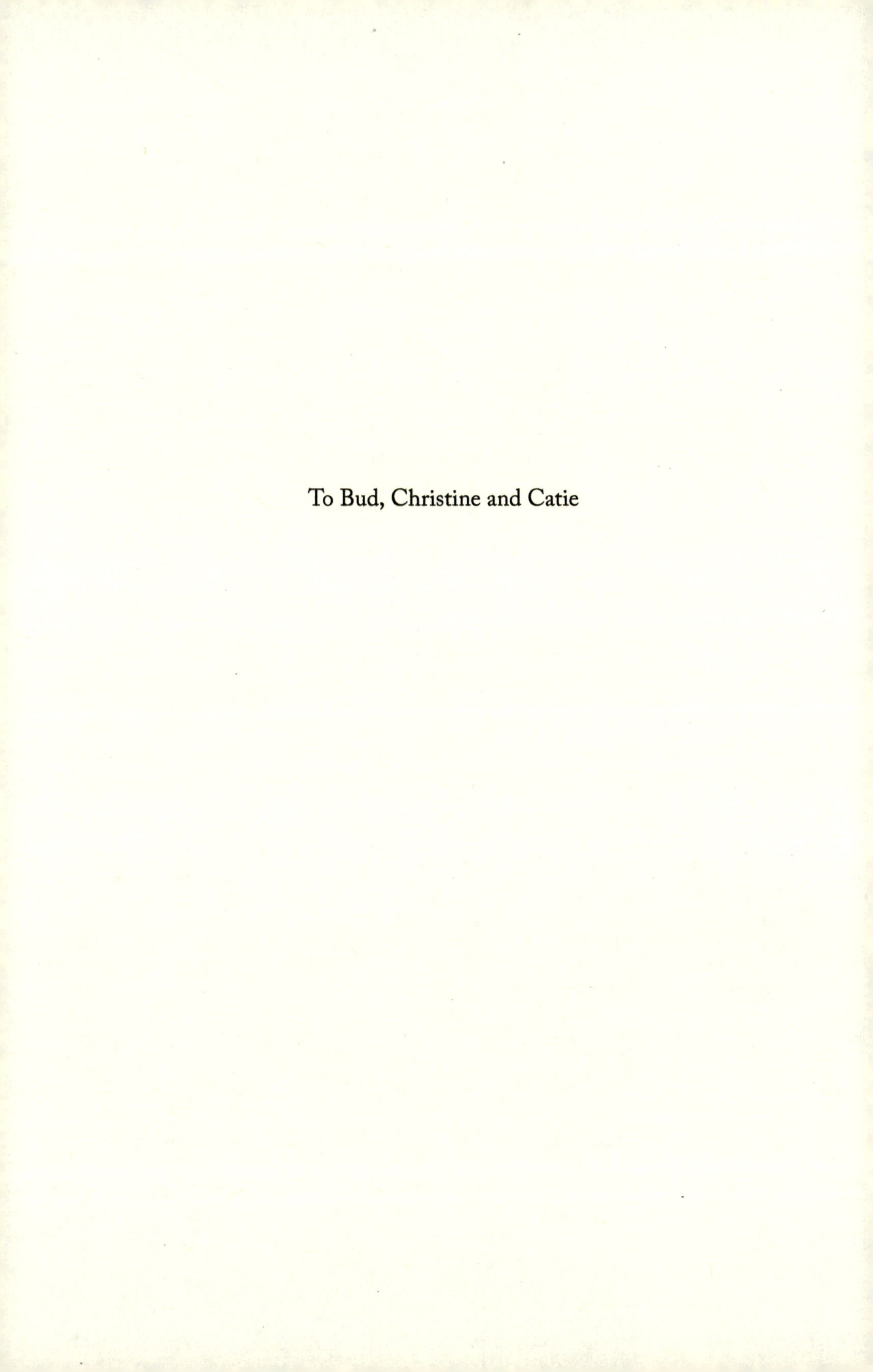

To Bud, Christine and Catie

“To know oneself, is above all, to know what one lacks.
It is to measure oneself against the Truth,
and not the other way around.”

Flannery O’Connor, “The Fiction Writer and His Country”

CHAPTERS

Preface 1

Chapter One - Just Married 3

Chapter Two - Guatemala 9

Chapter Three - Back Home 17

Chapter Four - At Work 23

Chapter Five - Parallels 25

Chapter Six - Love 31

Chapter Seven - People's Stories 37

Chapter Eight - Joy 39

Chapter Nine - Peace 45

Chapter Ten - Patience 51

Chapter Eleven - Kindness 55

Chapter Twelve - Goodness 61

Chapter Thirteen - Faithfulness 65

Chapter Fourteen - Gentleness 71

Chapter Fifteen - Self-Control 75

Chapter Sixteen - Logic 79

Conclusion 85

PREFACE

Everyone has a story, but few think much about their story or bother to tell it. Sadly, many people are out of touch with their own stories. Try asking someone for their story. This may prompt a confused look, followed by a muddled or incoherent response. This book was written in part to encourage readers to be aware of their own stories and how they evolve over time.

What makes a story? Length is immaterial; it can be long or short. A story is not just about events, for it is not what happened to you that matters, but how you respond to what happened. Even if we cannot control the course of events, we are always in control of our responses to those events. Some of those responses are life changing, which is why everybody's story is interesting. It describes who a person has become.

Your story is never finished. It is the work of a lifetime. Therefore, there is never one perfect time of life to tell your story, and no matter when you tell it you will still be writing it. Why did I choose to write this story now? I recently stumbled upon a useful organizing principle to provide a framework and coherence. My story is about many things, but not about all things. I believe that writing an authentic story about your life is not just about what you have to say but avoiding saying unimportant things.

The Early Train condenses events into two weeks, though they were actually experienced over the last several years. With the exception of the train conductor, Paul, all the characters and events are real, although names have been changed. Some of the footnotes are literary or biblical references, and some give credit to comments of friends or others who became part of this journey to one degree or another. Some of these people were just casual acquaintances, which testifies to the power of the right words spoken at the right time.

One final word of encouragement. We are always in the process of becoming, a process which is unique for each of us. You have work ahead which no one else can do. For this you have been hired, and from it you cannot be fired or retired, and the more you become, the more will be asked of you. Success is always at hand, even if it is sometimes hard to recognize. Like the signs on a train station platform, success achieved or failure recognized (another form of success) indicate progress as you speed toward your final destination.

CHAPTER ONE

JUST MARRIED

It was a fine June morning. The rising sun caught the railroad tracks at just the right angle to read the manufacturer's inscription: "Lackawanna Works 1974". The Lackawanna steel mill closed soon after that rail was installed here in Greenwich, Connecticut; long before Jonah moved east to enter the work force. A seasoned commuter for 30 years, Jonah was older than most passengers and one of the few boarding the 6:06 a.m. local train on pilgrimage to Grand Central Terminal.

As the sun rose, its light reflected brilliantly off two identical three-story office buildings opposite the railroad tracks. Built around the same time as railway station, the offices were originally leased by an emerging Greenwich business class traveling to New York City. But a new generation appropriated these offices for an opposite purpose. Young securities traders and arbitrageurs commuted from New York City to Greenwich, now acclaimed as "the hedge fund capital of the world." With more than $200 billion of hedge assets under management in just these two office buildings, the designation was well-deserved.

Up the hill along Greenwich Avenue, in contrast to the office towers, buildings still retained some charm of an old New England town, although the family owned markets and shops had long since been replaced by national brand stores. Window displays beckoned the well-to-do with such luxuries as communications and computing paraphernalia from Apple, zero-to-sixty-in-3.6 seconds cars from Tesla, and torn jeans from Ralph Lauren.

Jonah preferred the emptiness of the 6:06 train to the cramped quarters of an express. Most investment bankers swarmed onto the 5:59 express to reach their offices early, hoping to gain a competitive edge. Or they took the next express train at 6:37 to enjoy another 38 minutes of leisure. Investment banking is hard business, a young man's business, and the express trains are packed with younger men (and a few women). Jonah reckoned he stopped being a young man at age 50 and so accepted lesser compensation for a rewarding but less grueling vocation in finance.

At the age of 59, Jonah wanted more time for reflection, a valuable commodity unavailable on the express train. The extra ten minutes on the local train seemed more richly spent than at his desk.

The 6:06 was usually on time because so few people board further up-the-line. But not this day, as work crews repaired winter damage to ensure one more year of service to Lackawanna-1974. Four minutes late, the 6:06 local emerged a quarter mile east around the tree-lined bend. Jonah boarded and found a window seat in the rear of the train, the most vacant section of a largely vacant train.

Jonah usually allowed his mind to wander for two or three minutes until the dense foliage passing outside his window gave way to views of freeways and buildings, marking the last miles before entering New York State. The quiet emptiness of the car afforded reflective moments which would soon be extinguished by the cacophony of the city. The train slowed to receive a few riders waiting at Port Chester station, the first stop inside the New York State line. Seven more stops to Grand Central.

Jonah heard the slam of the double doors separating the train cars. He expected to see Solomon, the conductor for the back cars, a large, powerful looking deep voiced man and a fixture aboard the early train for many years. The new, unfamiliar figure entering the car was the antithesis of Solomon – short with a slight build, but older with mostly gray hair and weathered features of a man who has worked hard and seen much, carrying burdens largely unseen by others. His conductor's uniform was wrinkled and at least a size too large. Yet he moved with the assurance and grace of a man experienced in the job. The conductor surveyed the car, empty except for Jonah in his customary seat in the exit row window seat. He strolled slowly down the aisle and asked Jonah for his ticket.

Jonah flashed his monthly train pass to the conductor. "Where's Solomon today? Taking Friday off? Beautiful day for it."

"He was promoted, so I'll be filling in for a few days."

"Promoted?" Jonah replied. "At his age? He's worked the early train as long as I can remember."

"Yes, indeed. Served faithfully for many years. Good of you to have become acquainted with him."

"What's your name?"

"Paul".

Well, I'm Jonah, and I reckon I'll see you every day on this train for as long as you're filling in."

"Indeed, Jonah. Indeed." The conductor managed the faint yet unforced smile of a humble man who is naturally comfortable around people. He continued to the rear of the car as Jonah redirected his attention toward the passing scenery.

The more urban New York State scenery did not particularly interest Jonah having ridden this same route hundreds of times during all four seasons. Marking the scenery felt like marking time. Jonah was often asked how he could endure this commute after so many years, to which he would reply that it was productive time devoted to office matters just as easily studied on a train as at a desk. This dismissive remark applied well enough to the ride home but revealed nothing about the meditations of the morning trip.

These meditations usually began by reading a Bible passage, used as much to divert attention from window gazing as any kind of spiritual devotion. But this week was different; Jonah had married the week before for the second time. Ruth brought an irresistible light and life to the marriage, complementing Jonah's more worldly gifts of administration and analytical thought.

The marriage seemed improbable, for there was little in their pasts which should bring them together. However, many months prior, a woman in their church congregation approached Jonah and without any preliminary conversation stated plainly, "You will meet a woman next month who will become your wife." That was all. No elaboration or further discussion. The following month came and went with no event or experience which could possibly validate the prophesy, so Jonah put the matter out of his mind. Nor had he shared this word with Ruth, until soon after their wedding when he remembered the prophesy.

Jonah recalled first meeting Ruth. It was a brief and completely forgettable encounter among a group of 18 people gathered for dinner, and they shared no further interaction for several weeks until accidental circumstances brought them together again. Following marriage, Jonah related the prophecy to his church Pastor who seemed unsurprised. The Pastor explained that the woman who had approached Jonah with her vision was known to have a gift of prophesy.

Ruth seemed to share good cheer with everyone, from her best friends to strangers waiting in line at a hot dog stand. She was a part time-clown, and Jonah wondered if Ruth's good nature led her to clowning, or whether it was the other way around. Based on one week of marriage Jonah attributed it to a combination of native good nature and strong faith. Although naturally shy, Ruth's kindness and unpretentious nature attracted others to her who usually parted better off for the experience. As one of Ruth's closest friends once explained to Jonah, Ruth had a highly developed sense of mercy. Jonah reflected on the difference between mercy and ordinary run-of-the-mill kindness, but decided it didn't matter. Ruth was just Ruth. But, Jonah's mind could not let the question go that easily, for he believed that words really have precise meanings and should not be exchanged in a verbal flea market. Casual, unreflective expression comes at a cost of misunderstanding.

Whether mercy or kindness, it was what led Ruth to sign up Jonah and herself for a group mission trip to Guatemala scheduled soon after their wedding. This was Ruth's idea, but it wasn't Jonah's vision of a honeymoon. Ruth had proposed the trip during the course of planning for the wedding, which seemed to Jonah like a very bad time to appear reluctant and ungenerous, especially considering the desperate needs of that poor country. Jonah consented, though he remained unapologetically an American homebody traveling to a potentially unwelcoming outpost. They would leave Monday.

Jonah was relieved of these thoughts by the picturesque distraction outside. The train passed over the bridge connecting the Bronx and Manhattan boroughs, a stunning sight at dawn when the sun, still low but brilliant in the sky, skipped the length of the Harlem River, the last natural force between shores surrendered to concrete and steel. Soon, all sunlight was lost as the train entered the tunnel under Park Avenue for the final approach into Grand Central Terminal.

It was about a quarter-mile walk and three sets of stairs from the train platform to the terminal's north end exit at 48th Street and Park Avenue. It was a beautiful day, so every east/west cross street was bathed in a long light corridor from the sun rising over the East River. The temperature was cool but warming quickly, and Jonah was slightly disappointed that his walk was so short, just four blocks up to his office at 52nd Street and Park.

Jonah crossed Park Avenue and turned north. He turned west at 51st Street with a view toward cutting through an office building (where there was a Starbucks) that opened up onto both 51st and 52nd.

Jonah noticed a man apparently of Asian descent standing by the curb up ahead looking his way. As Jonah approached more closely he could see the man, casually but very presentably dressed, holding a paper cup seeking deposits from passersby. Panhandlers were an unremarkable sight in New York City, but this man's gaze met Jonah's eyes without flinching and with a peacefulness uncommon to panhandlers who typically exhibited either pushiness or complete indifference to others.

The man said nothing as Jonah passed without contributing. About five steps later Jonah felt a small pang of regret, or stinginess by another name. Compelled by second thoughts, he turned to go back only to see that the Asian man had vanished. The street was empty of cars and pedestrians at this early hour, and there was no building entrance within a hundred feet and it was even further back to Park Avenue. In short, there seemed no way the man could move out of eyesight within five seconds.

Motivated as much by curiosity as anything else, Jonah walked back to Park Avenue to look for the man. There was no one. Except one – a one legged man leaning on crutches with a cup in his hand. Jonah still felt a little guilty about ignoring the Asian man, so he considered compensating for the benefit of the one-legged man. He was a heavy set fellow, about 40-ish, perhaps Latino. Unlike other panhandlers, who almost always preferred to sit leaning against a building, this crippled man remained vertical, frequently adjusting his crutches into more comfortable positions under his arms. Jonah offered a clipped "g'morning" and two singles in the cup. The man replied with a wide smile and a vigorous nod of assent.

Jonah walked the last block up Park Avenue to work, still puzzling over the missing Asian man.

CHAPTER TWO

GUATEMALA

Departure day for the Guatemala mission trip arrived. Jonah had considered this more a tour than a mission trip since hands-on labor and assistance would be limited.

All fourteen participants were booked on the same flight from New York's Kennedy airport. They would connect in Houston on the second leg bound for Guatemala City. In the boarding area, the three participants who had visited Guatemala previously explained what to expect in the journey ahead. One of those three was Ruth, so Jonah was more familiar than most of the travelers about what to expect. Frequently recurring adjectives like "poor, welcoming, destitute, hopeful, dangerous and beautiful" made sense individually, but seemed incoherent in the whole. Jonah's own research revealed that Guatemala was one of the poorest countries in the world, with over half the population living below the poverty line. Families with a member working in the U.S. to help support the household were common. Expatriates annually returned over $9 billion to Guatemala, equaling about 12% of gross domestic product.

Before leaving Greenwich, Jonah had told each of his three children that he would be incommunicado in Guatemala for a few days. His son, Carl, a former Navy SEAL had remarked: "Guatemala is a beautiful country." Jonah was not aware that Carl had ever been anywhere in South America, and when asked, Carl replied: "Is this public? Not sure. But, we were helping the Guatemalan army blow up meth labs in the mountains." (This turned out to be an open secret in Guatemala. Most evenings during Jonah's trip the evening quiet would be broken by the sound of helicopters flying low and dark overhead dispatched, according to the mission group's host, to blow up meth labs.)

Jonah felt a yearning for the United States even before the group's connecting flight out of Houston had departed Bush International Airport. Following take-off the plane circled in the Houston night sky to point south. The aircraft leveled off in the darkness above the Gulf of Mexico, leaving the Houston City lights glimmering in the distant rear. Jonah craned his neck to catch a last glimpse of American land and felt strangely homesick.

Landing in Guatemala City, the mission group passed through customs and immigration without incident. They were met by their genial host and guide, Rafi. Now a devout Christian missionary, Rafi had an outlaw past with violent credentials. Perhaps as a reminder from whence he came, Rafi kept a 14–inch blade sword, still razor-sharp, and still holstered in its handsome leather crafted tasseled scabbard.

The route out of Guatemala City airport appeared similar to that of many cities with congested access roads crowded inside densely populated neighborhoods. Their destination (and Rafi's own neighborhood) was a good forty minutes from the airport. It was late evening so traffic was light. The further they drove, the street lighting grew dimmer and more prosperous areas gave way to third world slums. Gradually, all street life disappeared, even along four-lane roads lined with small commercial shops in marked contrast to other parts of the city. Rafi accelerated the bus from about 40 mph to about 60, which concerned the passengers. Rafi also appeared more alert and slightly tense which induced an uneasy quiet throughout the bus. Not wanting to alarm the mission group, Rafi explained without being asked that the bus would very soon pass out of the danger zone.

This was not a good sign. Rafi's neighborhood was known to be a poor neighborhood, so what reassurance was there that the bus would emerge into a safer locale? But, the American gringos had not anticipated the plucky resolve of the indigenous poor, who had built for themselves at great expense a walled compound four blocks square. There was only one entrance, which was armed by two paramilitary looking citizens armed with automatic rifles slung from their shoulders. Rafi stopped the bus, waved to the guards, greeted them in Spanish, and the gate opened. The bus rolled slowly into the community along a road barely wide enough for two subcompact cars to pass. The homes lining the street were extremely modest , but impeccably neat with an occasional garden. Rafi pointed with pride at the neighborhood school, which doubled as a church on Sundays. Rafi was the church Pastor.

The bus rolled to a stop in front of what would be the mission group's quarters for five days – two makeshift bunk houses, one for the men, and one for the women. Jonah and Ruth were assigned to the honeymoon suite – a school class room with a queen-sized blow-up mattress on the floor. Rafi explained that Jonah and Ruth would not interfere with classes inasmuch as students would not arrive until 8:00 a.m. by which time the mission group would be well on their way.

Jonah and Ruth struggled to keep from rolling off the air mattress which resisted flattening into a shape which could accommodate two people. Jonah gave up and slept that first night on the linoleum floor.

The first two days in Guatemala were fairly enjoyable as the neighbors went out of their way to welcome their guests and show hospitality by preparing meals for the group and even doing their laundry! Jonah was pleasantly surprised. He enjoyed travelling to interesting places marked by happy encounters with locals mostly known to Rafi. The mission group received unexpected favor from one mountain top community who enjoyed the use of a cinder block schoolhouse built by a youth group organized by Jonah's church in the prior year.

Day three into the trip brought the group face-to-face with harsher realities. The drive to Guatemala's main national cemetery passed through pleasant neighborhoods. Spread over several acres, the cemetery was well groomed and shaded from the late morning heat by rows of eucalyptus, jacaranda, and palm trees. Large monuments of apparently prominent former citizens dominated one section of the cemetery, while headstones belonging to citizens of more modest means populated an adjacent area. The least expensive graves were in huge above-ground walls holding up to a hundred coffins inserted like drawers. Several well-known people in Guatemalan history were buried here, which suggested a possible reason for the group's visit. A history lesson appeared to be in store, courtesy of Mike, an expatriate American guide recruited by Rafi for this occasion.

Mike was conversant in Guatemalan history, and Jonah was surprised to learn of American involvement here in the last century. It was a sad tale of how foreigners' taste for the simple banana produced a bitter harvest of autocratic government and elitist economic policies which promoted a permanent underclass and a seething social unease.

This dual class social structure extended even beyond death. Many graves were impermanent resting places, leased to families who could not afford to own even a hole in the ground. A body lying six feet under could rest in peaceful repose for as long as his family above ground kept the lease current. But, woe to the uncreditworthy corpse, for his remains are exhumed and his bones harvested for storage in the nearby ossuary with other delinquent skeletons. Sadly, no further use would be found for the empty coffin, which would be unceremoniously discarded over a cliff marking the cemetery's boundary.

Jonah felt an urge to peer over the cliff. A 400-foot vertical drop ends in the city dump, a 40-acre wasteland below the cemetery greenery. Directly below are the shattered remains of discarded coffins. Unlike American dumps where garbage is processed, here it is collected. Dozens of scavengers, known as Guajeros, roam the grounds picking through refuse seeking any item which might be repaired, cleaned and resold for the price of a meal. This task would be unpleasant enough in any dump, but it is especially distasteful in Guatemala where toilet tissue is discarded in wastebaskets due to inadequate plumbing. The air and grounds are toxic with scattered fires fueled by chemical waste. Jonah searched his heart for empathy or at least merciful feelings, but it comes harder when the subjects of your sympathy are so far below your feet as to look like ants crawling the grounds. Jonah tried to imagine the poverty that would reduce people to such penury and desperation, but it was too far outside his American experience.

The mission group walked slowly and silently back to the bus, feeling much less like missionaries in any meaningful sense of the word. Jonah struggled with two conflicting feelings, one to help the dump scavengers and the other a desire to return to the United States. This was only day three, so there was more to see.

Mike perched himself on the top step at the front of the bus, directing the driver to the next stop. Jonah felt relieved to be back on the city streets until the bus veered off a busy thoroughfare onto a cramped side road only wide enough for the bus. The street was lined with one- or two-room stucco houses. The street and home fronts were mostly tidy, although signs of long deferred upkeep were apparent for most homes.

This was a dead-end street, and the bus rolled to a stop facing the last house. Mike was the first off the bus with other passengers following, not having any idea who they were to visit or why. Possibly Mike had just lost his way and might be asking directions.

Mike knocked on the door, which was promptly opened by a very old woman in a well-worn flower print dress. Mike greeted the woman with a hug, a kiss on the cheek and a gentle Spanish salutation. He then turned to the group and introduced Consuela who grinned with a welcoming smile. She did not speak any English so Mike explained that Consuela had graciously agreed in advance to display the wares of her trade. Consuela returned briefly inside the house and returned with two small dolls, wonderfully crafted, neatly painted and cutely dressed. Mike explained that the dolls were reconstructed from discards at the municipal dump from which the group came. Consuela was more than a professional scavenger; she was an artisan engaged in a craft of sufficient market value to support the life style of a free standing home, however modest.

Mike asked Consuela if she would pose in a picture with the group. She shyly gave her consent. The photo op also served as a convenient way to say goodbye and board the bus. Every passenger felt surprisingly blessed by the unexpected encounter with a woman who had virtually nothing to give except a smile and her goodwill.

The rising sun streamed through the window of the "honeymoon suite" on day four, waking Jonah and Ruth. The mission group arose at 6:30 a.m. so as to be ready for the 7:30 departure Rafi had announced the night before. They were expected early because the first stop was to be at a school in a low section of the city called La Limonada. La Limonada was named for the lemon groves which so beautifully covered the area decades before. The lemon groves disappeared during the 36-year civil war which began in 1954 as refugees began settling there to escape the brutal violence of guerilla and government forces.

Today, La Limonada is home to 60,000 to 100,000 people and is the largest urban slum in Central America. It is considered a "red zone", a designation reserved for Guatemala's poorest and most dangerous communities. Early morning is thought to be the safest time of day, though no time is a safe time in La Limonada.

The sky was cloudless and the temperature was already in the mid-70s, so this promised to be a hot day. Fortunately, the inland areas around Guatemala City had dry climates, unlike the more humid coastal zones.

As a weekday commuter, Jonah was accustomed to train schedules and timely departures. Accordingly, Jonah and Ruth arrived at the curb promptly at 7:28 a.m., alone. By 7:40 three others had arrived, but no Rafi and no bus. By 7:45 half the mission group had congregated at the curb. Jonah grew impatient. Suddenly Jonah heard Rafi's unmistakable laugh echo from the meal room across the street where the sounds of breakfast plates being stacked and cleared could be heard through the open windows.

Jonah opened the screen door to the meal room to find Rafi sitting among tables filled with assorted local friends and mission group members in casual conversation, full coffee cups in hand. Now in a huff, Jonah exclaimed, "I thought wheels up was at 7:30!"

Unruffled, with an innocence shared by all peoples unaccustomed to time schedules, Rafi glanced toward the door. "We have plenty of time," he said. The expressions of others in the room suggested nothing out of the ordinary and conversation continued as before. One of the diners leaned over to Jonah and explained: "This is Guatemala time."

The group finally boarded the bus at 8:35 and rolled out of the compound. La Limonada is within the Guatemala City limits, normally about a half hour drive, but almost twice that during rush hour. (Some Guatemalans like to arrive at work on time.) By now the group's shared experience had reinforced a bond which made it easy to fill idle time with conversation. Accordingly, the traffic tedium was relieved by one traveler who held forth on the theological underpinnings of the term "Holy Cow." This led into an absurd peroration on the origins of "Holy Toledo" and "Holy Moly."

The city streets narrowed as the bus entered La Limonada, which was less a neighborhood than buildings thrown together with no apparent thought to municipal design or practicality. Most structures had no more than one small window facing the street as if to present the most uninviting face to ward off unwelcome visitors. Still, this was the high rent district of La Limonada.

Somehow, the driver found a plot of flat cement large enough to accommodate the bus and parked near the local grade school. As the group filed into the school, laughing students were already scurrying from first-period classes to second-period classes. Rafi explained that the students were happiest during school hours (not necessarily a common sentiment among American students) because the school building was perhaps the safest place in the community. Two teachers briefly presented to the group wherein they spoke of the challenges of educating children in a desperately poor and violent community where every family is subject to hardship and tragedy. These conditions are also a source of shame for the residents, so young people seeking employment provide false home addresses.

These remarks were illuminating, but insufficient to prepare the group for what they would see next. The bus could go no deeper into La Limonada, so the group walked in a tight group behind Rafi into a sprawling camp of residential shacks constructed with corrugated steel sheets. Each structure was barely high enough for a man of average height to clear. Several homes had only three sides, with perhaps a blanket serving as a fourth wall.

Some homes had toilets, but no plumbing. Other homes had no toilets and no plumbing. Natural water streams which in former times had fed the lemon groves but had since become putrid makeshift sewers rushed through deep crevices among the shacks. The more fortunate residents of La Limonada resided at the higher regions where the streams were only somewhat discolored and the stench fairly bearable, though the less fortunate residents lower in the ravine had to contend with the accumulated sewage of their neighbors above.

Rafi had arranged for the group to visit a resident at his home which, like most others, consisted of a single room open to the air on one side. They were introduced to Miguel, an infirm widower who now lived alone. He welcomed the group into his home, but a large bed took up most of the available space so most stood just outside where the fourth wall would have been.

The resident of course spoke no English, so Rafi translated. Miguel had fought on the government's side in the civil war. When the war ended in 1990 he had no money and physical disabilities made him unqualified for the only work available. To say he and his wife moved to La Limonada would imply that the couple had belongings worth moving. It would be more accurate to say that they found a recently vacated shack whose resident had just passed away. Thankfully, a fellow army member (with the help of his old service rifle) stood guard over the newly available space until Miguel and his wife could arrive to defend their own space on the hillside. They had lived there ever since, until Miguel's wife died of an unknown ailment several years prior.

Now alone, ailing and completely indigent, Miguel nevertheless exuded a certain peace. Rafi asked if he would like anything from the group. Miguel considered the request thoughtfully, his reply translated by Rafi, "A song?" He replied. "Can anyone sing a song?"

Jonah considered what he had seen on days three and four, the plight of the scavengers and the residents of La Limonada. This was unrelenting poverty, unrelieved by mercy and justice. But, mercy is professed by many and practiced by few, so it is drained away long before it can reach the slums of Guatemala which is left only with the ghastly streams coursing among the unfortunate. Justice here is controlled by few and dispensed to few.

Witnessing hardship on this scale was a new experience for Jonah. He wondered if he would lapse into indifference over time. Perhaps, if he remembered it as simply hardship. Perhaps not if he considered its effect in suffering. It is easy to be overtaken by one's own hardships in the course of daily life, but suffering consumes us. Yet, the poor of Guatemala appeared surprisingly resilient. That resilience might be remembered either as a hopeful example, or as mere managed hardship. Jonah realized his instincts tended toward the latter, but his heart contemplated the former.

CHAPTER THREE

BACK HOME

Day five was departure day, and even Rafi conceded to timetables where airline flights were concerned. The importance of air travel from Guatemala was rooted in the country's business history from the 19th and early 20th century when it was the financial center of Central America. Banking and commerce depended on access to transportation which was honored in the present day by serviceable airport facilities and ample access to foreign airlines. Today, the bus to Guatemala City airport left on time.

The Guatemala experience seemed far away to Jonah as he took his familiar spot on the Greenwich train platform. The Monday morning sun still rode the familiar rail, "Lackawanna Works 1974". Jonah was grateful for that rail. It exuded stability in a changing world and strength in a society where the foundations were threatened. Jonah would remember Guatemala as neither stable nor strong, but his experience left him suspicious of the permanence of any social system not assiduously maintained in the present and nurtured for the future. He remembered that even the great Lackawanna Works collapsed almost 40 years ago.

It was easy to think of what America had which Guatemala lacked. Too easy. In a land of plenty we lose count of blessings without burdensome thoughts of virtues lacking. But today felt different. Jonah was more aware of sins and temptations common to man, whether he be Guatemalan or American. Where was mercy in La Limonada, in the Guatemala City dump, or at the corner of 51st & Park? Jonah could avoid the thousands in Guatemala City, but probably not the one-legged man one block from his office.

The 6:06 train rounded the last bend heading into Greenwich station and pulled alongside the platform. The rear train doors opened revealing an empty car. Jonah slumped down in his customary window seat in the exit row. The train slowly accelerated out of Greenwich station. Moments later, the conductor passed through the forward doors and scanned the car for passengers. It had been a week since Jonah last rode the early train, but he recognized Paul's thin frame and weathered features.

A beam of recognition flashed across Paul's face. "Welcome back, Jonah. Where've you been?"

"Guatemala."

"That so?" replied Paul. "What did you think?"

Jonah reflected for a moment. He glanced at Paul to discern if he was really curious about what he thought or whether he was just making conversation. He did his best to come up with a one-sentence impression: "It makes you think about mercy," Jonah ventured.

"Mercy?"

Jonah figured he picked the wrong word. "Yeah, mercy."

"You mean, as in kindness"?

"I guess so. I think they are about the same thing." Jonah figured Paul would accept that as a sensible end to the conversation.

"Not quite, Jonah"

"What do you mean?"

"Well," replied Paul, " Mercy leads to kindness all right. Has to. Mercy isn't mercy unless it comes out somehow. But it doesn't always work in reverse."

"I'm not sure I follow."

"There are other reasons to be kind, such as to impress someone or to get what you want from somebody. Or, in other cases, maybe it just comes naturally to some folks."

"I never looked at it that way before," replied Jonah.

"Don't take my word for it. Look it up, Jonah. After all, how many hundreds of times does the Bible refer to mercy?"

"Are you a Bible scholar or something, Paul? Where would you look?"

"I suppose you could start with Googling the best mercy reference you can find. The internet is good for that. You know, the most hits rise to the top and all that. Then look for context and maybe associations and parallels just fall right out in front of you."

Paul turned back toward the forward doors before Jonah could ask any more. The train was pulling into Port Chester, NY.

Jonah felt unsatisfied by his conversation with Paul, as if having just half an answer. He returned intermittently to consider the matter during the remainder of the ride to Grand Central, but the train noise resounding in the Grand Central tunnel disrupted his thoughts. Jonah left the train with the question unresolved.

Jonah passed the same Starbucks coffee shop every day on his way up Park Avenue. Jonah usually settled for the free coffee in the office kitchen, but once in a while he would treat himself to a Grande Bold at Seattle's finest. The sun was shining and life seemed good, so this was one of those days.

Even at 7:00 a.m. a line was already forming at the counter. But, the baristas processed requests with dispatch so coffee was soon in hand. Jonah walked over to the side table, covered his coffee with a lid and slipped on a corrugated sleeve.

"Excuse me, sir", came a young woman's voice. Jonah looked to his right to see who had addressed him. It was one of the baristas. "Would you work for me today? The day has been hard, and I have a long day ahead."

Jonah figured this for typical Monday morning banter, but the woman was not smiling. He regarded the woman closely. She was an attractive brunette, probably early twenties, well turned out with a Starbucks apron covering a clean white shirt and black tights. Jonah studied her eyes, which remain fixed on him with no indication that this was a joke. He paused, baffled and unsure what to say, expecting the woman to offer more of an explanation. Jonah felt uncomfortable. There was no way for the discussion to continue without venturing into a private personal space, a place where Jonah was unequipped and reluctant to enter. It was one thing to sympathize with the one legged man on 51st and Park, because the nature of any transaction with him is anticipated and involved little conversation beyond "have a nice day." But it was quite another to be thrust into a personal conversation with a complete stranger.

The pause was filled by no further information, which added to the tension. Jonah broke the silence. "I'm afraid I cannot work for you, because I have work of my own to do today."

This response seemed stilted and cold compared to the personal beginning of the exchange. The barista said nothing and looked at the floor, but did not move. There was no indication of whether she had accepted Jonah's explanation, but she conveyed an air of resignation as if giving in to low expectations.

Jonah was at a loss to respond to the barista in a helpful way, or even in a sympathetic way! In the office he would receive the honors of a working man where performance can exceed expectations, but where are the honors of the Christian man?

Jonah arrived in the office a few minutes later than usual. As he waited for his computer to boot up he stared into his coffee. It tasted strangely bitter. Should have ordered Pike, he guessed. This would be a busy day. Assets under management were growing nicely owing to a steady increase in clients and rising markets. Wealth management was a late life career for Jonah. He had spent twenty years as an investment banker, but that was a young man's business, and he unofficially stopped being a young man at fifty. Jonah loved the mystery of markets, so he had joined a large hedge fund which was seeding new strategies. After a promising start, Jonah's strategy flat-lined. He had left the hedge fund, grateful for the opportunity, but feeling like a man deprived of oxygen. He had missed the stimulation of working with other people. Wealth management offered that stimulation in the form of clients... if he could just find some clients.

He had found some. Or, rather they found him.

Jonah had marketed himself earnestly and purposefully to people he knew well, those most likely to trust him and believe that his former skills could be harvested for this new purpose. He had written every letter and made every call with no result whatsoever. Jonah had expected a slow ramp, but this was no ramp at all and he was out of ideas. He recalled staring at his phone. It had three lines, but they were all dark. In that quiet moment Jonah had lifted up a prayer: "Great Lord, I thought You had opened a door into this new business, and I have tried to be faithful in doing all I could do, but it has come to nothing. If You want me to stay in this business, You will have to take the next step."

Never in all Jonah's experience had a prayer been answered instantly and with such clear effect. The phone rang. Jonah answered the call of a former investment banking client who had just sold his business and needed help investing the proceeds. The client explained that Jonah was perhaps uniquely suited for this specialized need which involved developing a fixed income program which could absorb excess foreign tax credits. This was not just the first client, but a large client.

Jonah was well occupied for a time, but no new business emerged for several more weeks. Maybe the fixed income client was a fluke. Jonah was out of ideas again, so one more time he lifted up the prayer: "Great Lord, I had thought You had opened a door into this new business, and I have tried to be faithful in doing all I could do. But it has come to little. If You want me to stay in this business, You will have to take the next step." The telephone instantly came to life, and another even more promising client became part of Jonah's business.

It was early Saturday morning later that same month of the second phone call. Jonah was driving into downtown Greenwich to his favorite coffee shop on Greenwich Avenue when he felt a strange, compelling urge to turn left and head in the opposite direction on Route 1. He saw the familiar Starbucks up ahead, though he had rarely patronized it because it was located in a crowded shopping center. But, he was here now, so he might as well make an exception.

Before he could take his place in line, Jonah spotted an acquaintance seated with his coffee and an open Bible. They exchanged greetings. The friend was aware of Jonah's new occupation and wished him the customary good wishes, but then added the question: "What are you looking at now?" Jonah explained that the financial crisis of 2008-2009 had perverse effects on real (after-inflation) interest rates and the best way to take advantage of this (and with very little risk) was to buy U.S. Treasury Inflation Protected Securities. The friend said he had been considering the same thing, adding: "I will wire you $30 million first thing Monday morning." Thus ended a one-minute conversation.

And so it went. Everywhere Jonah looked for business he came up empty. All his business came from places he never looked.

CHAPTER FOUR

AT WORK

Tuesdays were usually busy days at the office, but today especially so. In addition to Jonah's normal work he had to prepare for a meeting with management for his annual business review scheduled for later that morning. His report would consist mostly of good news and good prospects, so he looked forward to the meeting.

The conference rooms were newly built with fresh contemporary furniture and walls adorned with large flat screens connected wirelessly to company data feeds capable of displaying account information, market data or other client presentation materials. Jonah and his business would be examined in a room capable of seating twelve people at a long, rectangular conference table. Two of the room's four sides were primarily glass, one side facing the central reception area and the opposite side affording a sunny southerly view of mid-town Manhattan.

Arnie, the manager, and Conrad, the assistant manager, were already in the conference room when Jonah arrived, having just completed another interview. Jonah was invited to take a seat opposite the assistant manager at the far end of the conference table. The manager sat at the head of the table at the opposite end. Clearly, the assistant manager would direct the discussion.

The meeting began with the usual pleasantries about nothing in particular, when Arnie suggested starting the meeting so as to keep on schedule. Jonah faced the assistant manager and waited for direction. After a pause, the Conrad spoke haltingly in a most distracted fashion, somewhat disengaged from the task at hand.

"Are you doing OK today?" Jonah asked.

"Maybe not as good as I would like," came the reply. Conrad did not lift his eyes from the papers in front of him.

Jonah considered asking Conrad what was wrong, but felt this might not be a sharing moment with Conrad's boss in the room. Instead he offered: "Would you mind if I prayed for you?" Jonah had no idea what to expect from this offer in a business meeting and half wished he had not brought it up.

"I'd like that," came the surprising response. "Do we all have to talk?"

"Not at all. Permit me." Jonah gathered himself. Following a moment's deep reflection, he offered: "Great Lord, we thank You for bringing us together in this great enterprise to do the work that You have given us to do, for You are in all work. Accordingly, we ask Your blessing on all who labor here, especially Arnie, our manager and Conrad, our assistant manager, and that you may supply whatever is lacking to accomplish Your purposes. Finally, we ask that you attend to any special needs which Conrad or any of us in this room may have this day. In Jesus's name we pray, Amen."

The momentary quiet in the conference room was one of reflection, not awkwardness. Arnie spoke from the far end of the table, "That felt really good!"

The meeting proceeded thereafter in a normal fashion and concluded on time.

CHAPTER FIVE

PARALLELS

As Jonah boarded the early train, he reflected on the prior day's meeting with management. It yielded no new insights into the wealth management business, but did suggest something about prayer. The popular culture does not believe in prayer, but few people refuse it when it is offered by another.

Paul emerged from the forward car and Jonah suddenly recalled their last conversation regarding mercy. He knew Paul was going to ask him about it.

"Did you look it up?" Paul asked as he punched the seat ticket.

"No. Maybe I'll do it now on my phone before I forget," replied Jonah as Paul returned to the forward car.

Jonah Googled "mercy," which returned 325 million results. Tops on this very long list were hospitals and health organizations, followed closely by music titles and TV shows. The first page of the search even included a site discussing mercy for animals.

Jonah paused to consider how best to narrow the search. He tried "mercy Jesus" figuring that if Jesus could not produce mercy, nobody could. This produced much more promising results, among which was a site entitled: "What does the Bible say about mercy?" Jonah clicked on the link which identified some of the many places in the Bible where mercy is mentioned. Among those featured was a reference to the Sermon on the Mount. Jonah recognized this as one of the most famous Bible passages, referred to by one commentator as "Jesus's Manifesto."

The Sermon on the Mount was almost three pages long in most print editions, but the most well-known segment was one paragraph long:

> "Blessed are the poor in spirit for theirs is the kingdom of heaven.
> Blessed are those who mourn, for they shall be comforted.
> Blessed are the meek, for they shall inherit the earth.
> Blessed are those who hunger and thirst for righteousness, for

> they shall be satisfied.
> Blessed are the merciful, for they shall receive mercy.
> Blessed are the pure in heart, for they shall see God.
> Blessed are the peacemakers, for they shall be called sons of God.
> Blessed are those who are persecuted for righteousness' sake, for theirs is the kingdom of heaven.
> Blessed are you when others revile you and persecute you and utter all kinds of evil against you falsely on my account. Rejoice and be glad, for your reward is great in heaven...."[1]

There it was – the fifth of nine blessings called the beatitudes: blessed are the merciful for they shall receive mercy. But this just seemed to define mercy in terms of itself without telling what mercy actually looked like. Paul had suggested looking at parallels, whatever that meant. Jonah tried thinking what merciful would line up with somewhere else, but then he would be back to where he started. But, what if the beatitudes as a group lined up with some other explanation somewhere else?

Jonah counted the beatitudes. There were nine. He knew that fours and sevens came up a lot in the Bible and there were the Ten Commandments, but he could not think of any "nines". He needed some different words to search related things. The only word he thought might mean mercy was the one he had suggested to Paul – kindness – was imperfect, but Jonah typed "kindness" into his Google search anyway, paused to think of a qualifier to narrow the search, and added "new testament." This returned a mere 13 million results. But, the very first page included an entry for "Fruit of the Spirit--Kindness," which seemed promising as he recalled that "fruit" in this context was actually a list of several things. Jonah hit the link.

An essay appeared from Good News Magazine[2]. It was a brief article, but cited an interesting study of 16,000 individuals around the world from 37 cultures in which people were asked their most desired traits in a mate. For both sexes, the first preference was kindness. The author cited further studies revealing that although people want to be treated kindly, they often have difficulty acting kindly themselves. So, here was at least one author who connected mercy with kindness.

---

1 Matthew 5:3-11

2 Don Hooser, "Fruit of the Spirit--Kindness" is a web publication at: ucg.org/the-good-news/the-fruit-of-the-spirit-from-the-heart-to-the-helping-hand

The article also provided a link to the fruit of the Spirit where they are listed in Galatians 5:22-23: "love, joy, peace, patience, kindness, goodness, faithfulness, gentleness, self control." Apparently, the fruit of the spirit has several aspects, nine, to be exact. Were these Paul's parallels? Jonah pulled the back page off an equity research report from his brief case, flipped it over to the blank side and scrawled a table with the beatitudes on one side and fruit of the Spirit on the other:

poor in spirit .... love
those who mourn .... joy
meek .... peace
hunger and thirst for righteousness .... patience
merciful .... kindness
pure in heart .... goodness
peacemakers .... faithfulness
persecuted for righteousness sake .... gentleness
persecuted for Jesus's sake .... self-control

Jonah's thoughts were interrupted when the train pulled into the Harrison, NY station and doors slammed behind Paul as he entered Jonah's car. Two passengers boarded the car, and as the train pulled out of Harrison Paul checked their tickets and walked past Jonah. "Hey, Paul. I was thinking about what you said about parallels. I never thought about this before, but it looks like there is a correspondence between the nine beatitudes and the nine fruit of the Spirit. Some line up perfectly, like mercy and kindness. But, some don't, like peacemakers and faithfulness. What do you think?"

"I think the question is: did the person who listed the fruit of the Spirit have the beatitudes in mind," replied Paul. "Just remember, the fruit of the Spirit do not operate separately. It is a coherent whole. That's why it's 'fruit' and not 'fruits.' God gave us a vision for being, not a list of errands."

Before Jonah had a chance to answer, Paul exited through the forward doors. If you are a conductor keeping a schedule your remarks are concise.

Paul raised a good question. Either the parallels between the nine beatitudes and the nine fruit of the Spirit were a complete accident (which seemed unlikely), or they were by design. If they were by design, then there had to be a rational connection between each and every pair, even if certain pairs were not connected in obvious ways.

Jonah would have to consider each pair separately, but he had little patience for that now that the train was already pulling into New Rochelle, one of the last stops before Grand Central. Besides, he had other questions, such as why are some really good qualities not fruit of the Spirit, like gratitude or courage? And, is the fruit of the Spirit just a simpler way to say what the beatitudes are? Or, on a practical level, how do you practice all those good things when life often just isn't working?

Jonah recalled someone saying that we ask God too many uninteresting and pointless questions. One time in prayer, as a test, he asked God: "God, what do you think of me?" The answer returned: "Act justly, love mercy and walk humbly with your God." *[3] His truths are plainer than our questions, and that answer seemed simpler than the beatitudes.

The beatitudes seemed a little dense and awkward. The fruit of the spirit sounds like a list of things everyone would want. All nine fruit are attractive attributes. But, Jonah wasn't sure he wanted much to feel the sentiments of the beatitudes. Who wants to be poor, mournful, meek, hungry and thirsty?

Jonah did not return to these thoughts until that night. As he slipped into bed the day's business receded from consciousness and the vacuum filled with things eternal. Though unresolved in his mind, they exerted a welcome calming influence as sleep enveloped him.

It has been said that dreams are illustrations from the book your soul is writing about you.[4] And so it was that Jonah found himself in an imaginary place, but one common to his experience, a country club in a lush setting. Jonah felt overdressed in his dark suit, pressed white shirt, repp tie and shined cap-toe shoes. He walked along a path bisecting a manicured lawn of emerald green. As he walked toward a tennis court the path grew narrower and became muddy. His shoes sunk into the mud above the souls as he passed the tennis court where four African-American women played doubles in their tennis whites. The path ended, and before him was more lawn stretching up a mild slope. The lawn seemed irresistibly inviting, so Jonah walked up the hill. He heard someone calling him in the distance to his left. He turned and saw a one-room shack, closed on three sides, but open on the side facing the lawn. Inside the shack was a very old woman in bed. She appeared to be in the last hours of life, and she called to

3 Micah 6:8

4 Marsha Norman, *The Fortune Teller.* New York: Bantam Books, 1988.

Jonah asking him to approach. Jonah pointed to the mud on his shoes as an explanation for keeping his distance.

This dream was followed by a second dream. Jonah approached the front door of a very large mansion. He knocked. A man opened the door and welcomed Jonah in a subdued tone. Jonah was invited in and he was led down a hall to a closed door on the left. Jonah was told he was expected and would be received inside the room. He entered. The room was completely empty, with no windows or doors other than the one through which he entered. The door closed behind Jonah leaving him in blackest darkness. Suddenly the entire wall opposite him shone with a searing brightness, yet the interior of the room remained dark and completely unilluminated. The brightness was irresistible to look at, yet impossible to do so for more than a split second. The wall filled with writing which scrolled rapidly from top to bottom. Jonah struggled to read the writing but the light forced him to divert his eyes.

Jonah awoke in a dazed state, unsure for a moment where he was. He was baffled by the two dreams and unable to interpret them, so he reached for a notepad on the bedside table to record what he could remember for future reference.

CHAPTER SIX

LOVE

The train platform affords a moment of forced pause, especially in the quiet of 6:00 a.m. A place where hundreds of commuters might stand two hours later is now deserted except for a handful of early risers at the front of the platform, and Jonah alone at the rear. The earliest morning riders are rewarded by sights of the occasional hawk, turkey vulture or owl perched on the building roofs opposite the platform. The late riders have only each other as company.

The early riders are an unhurried lot, content to wait unoccupied by cell phones or newspapers to observe the world around them. When else can you see the first light reflect off the town hall tower, or count the birds perched on the train pantograph wires? Even on the busiest commuter line in the country it is possible in this brief moment, to be unnoticed and alone with thoughts which go unexplored during the crush of the day.

So immersed was Jonah in his thoughts that he did not hear the approaching train until it rolled across his gaze. He boarded alone and found his usual window seat in the exit row. The tracks opposite the train allowed a parallel ride in the opposite direction. But, the parallel Jonah had in mind this morning almost surely moves in only one direction. The first beatitude ("poor in spirit") might engender love as the first fruit of the Spirit, but it was hard to imagine love causing one to be poor in spirit.

Jonah was not even sure what "poor in spirit" meant. Did it describe a feeling, or a condition, and would it be obvious to yourself or to others? Jonah imagined asking a random person how he was doing today, and hearing a response like: "well, rather poor in spirit, thank you." Such a response would have to mean something more than "OK" or "not so good."

Paul walked into the rear car, careful to keep at least one hand on a seat to steady himself on the moving train. "Paul," began Jonah, "I'm on just the first beatitude and I'm already stuck."

Paul replied, "Jesus said 'Good news is preached to the poor.'[5] Yet, He was as accessible to the rich as to the poor. So the distinction is not a socioeconomic one. Consider this. A poor person lacks what is needed to sustain life, and he is in a constant search to get what he needs. A poor person who needs money might look for well-off people for a loan or a hand-out. Similarly, a person who is poor in spirit would seek someone who is rich in spirit to get a refilling of spirit. The only person I can think of who has lots of spirit to give away is God. Some people give up at that point because God seems far away. Maybe, but maybe not. It says somewhere: 'I live in a high and holy place, but also with him who is contrite and lowly of spirit.'[6] If true, then such a person poor in spirit could be blessed indeed ."

Jonah considered that as Paul punched the seat ticket and walked on. He could imagine a debate among the religions of the world and self-help gurus about where we get a fresh infilling of spirit, but most seem to agree it doesn't come from your navel, but from something outside yourself. Paul spoke from a Christian perspective which seemed to say that a fresh infilling of spirit was readily available and free of charge to those who ask, and the first part of that ask is to admit your lack of it.

Perhaps that is how the first beatitude connects with the first fruit of the spirit, love. A person poor in spirit who admits he is poor would be humble because it is easier to love from a low place than a high place. But humility is not the definition of "poor in spirit." It is just a facet of it. Another facet is having a vision of what a high place looks like, a vision which works for every man, not just for some people from some culture at some time but something timeless and unchanging. Otherwise, it is just a vague notion, and you can't get an infilling of something you can't identify.

Paul returned to the rear car, so Jonah took the opportunity to continue where he left off. "Paul, suppose you don't think of yourself as poor in spirit because things are pretty good?

"Then, good for you!" replied Paul. "But, what are you pleased about, yourself or your circumstances? By all means, be glad in good circumstances. However, where you have grown pleased with yourself,

5 Matthew 11:5

6 Isaiah 57:15

there you shall remain."[7]

"OK," replied Jonah. "But on the other hand, being in a low place sounds a little like self-loathing."

"Even if we see ourselves in a low place a vision of a high place precludes self-loathing because it is aspirational. It is where to get more of what you need. Need for what? Need to love. So, being poor in spirit is where you start to get the capacity to love. So, love is a fruit of the spirit."

The train slowed as it pulled into New Rochelle station. The doors opened to admit commuters. More passengers boarded than normal and the rear car began filling up such that even the middle seats would be used. A 30-something African-American woman took the empty middle seat next to Jonah. She carried a stack of folders for work. On top was a children's picture book of Bible stories.

"Who is the book for?" Jonah asked.

"For me," replied the woman. "Sometimes the Bible is hard for me to understand, but this book is pretty simple."

This made sense to Jonah. "How is it written that makes it easier to understand?"

"Every section poses a question, and the question is followed by a story," replied the woman. "That's why kids love it, because they intuitively like stories. Their brains aren't so ready for abstract ideas, but the stories and the people are real to them. That approach works as well to understand everyday situations as it does to understand old Bible parables. That's because real people – every single one of us (even kids) – have real stories. So, this book helps me think in terms of people's stories. For example, when you saw folks board the train in New Rochelle, did you see commuters, or did you see people? People have stories. 'Commuter' is just a description of someone's weekday habit and limits the way we view them."

"So, you like to know people's stories?" replied Jonah.

"When possible," replied the woman, "because if you know their

---

7 St. Augustine, Sermon 169. "If *you* would attain to what *you are* not yet, *you* must always *be* displeased by what *you are*. For *where you are pleased with yourself there you have remained. Keep* adding, *keep* walking, *keep* advancing.".

stories, you know their cares. Knowing their cares is the first step to substituting the cares of someone else for your own cares, which is how love works. We are supposed to do that with potentially anyone, which is hard. That is why love is a commandment."

"And that's why we need to be refilled once in a while," added Jonah.

"Indeed," replied the woman.

"I'd feel uncomfortable horning my way into somebody's story without being invited."

"Don't go where you are not welcome," answered the woman. "But, love is not an emotion; it is something you do on purpose. So, if you see an opening and you don't take it, then maybe pride is in the way. So, take a shot. Failing in love is better than succeeding in pride. And, don't be intimidated by anyone high and mighty, because being significant is no substitute for being loved."

Jonah slumped into his seat and stared out the window over the Harlem River as he digested the woman's remarks. Maybe trains are more interesting than he thought. Maybe there are some interesting stories in this car. He looked at faces around him, but they disclosed nothing. There was an unwritten code of quiet on the early train, so he did not expect to be invited into anyone's life story.

Yet, the inescapable truth was that Christian doctrines without love are incoherent. Secular society has adopted many biblical rules (such as those prohibiting murder, theft, etc.), but they have done so selectively as one chooses from a menu. Some rules seem obvious, but personal convictions alone are poor substitutes for truth. Convictions ungirded by love make you obnoxious because the Bible is not about rules; it is about Jesus.

Society has become polite, but has lost the ability to love. For lack of love, even politeness is lost. Jonah would later reflect on a passage from a sermon by C.S. Lewis called "The Weight of Glory," which reads:

> "If you asked twenty good men today what they thought was the highest of the virtues, nineteen of them would reply, Unselfishness. But if you had asked almost any of the great Christians of old, he would have replied, Love. You see what happened? A negative term has been substituted

> for a positive, and this is of more than of philosophical importance. The negative idea of Unselfishness carries with it the suggestion not primarily of securing good things for others, but of going without them ourselves, as if our abstinence and not their happiness was the important point. I do not think this is the Christian virtue of Love. The New Testament has lots to say about self-denial, but not about self-denial as an end in itself."

The train pulled into Grand Central Terminal, and Jonah struggled to reorient himself to the tasks of the day ahead. Yet, he hung on to the thoughts developed on the train ride, for he believed them to be true. They could change the way he looked at work and those with whom he worked.

Jonah held these thoughts as he strolled up Park Avenue. The familiar one-legged man leaned on his crutches at the corner of Park and 51st Street. Jonah approached the man and asked his name. The man spoke either a foreign language or unintelligible English. Jonah wasn't sure which, but it sounded like his name might be John. Jonah introduced himself, which John understood to be John. So, each person shared a common name which belonged to neither one. Jonah found some singles in his wallet and buried them in the cup of One-Leg-John, a ritual Jonah would repeat frequently.

CHAPTER SEVEN

PEOPLE'S STORIES

The train rides home were always crowded, and this Thursday was no exception. Jonah looked around at other passengers and wondered about their stories, each one unique, and each one shaping his or her circumstances. Jonah wondered about the possibility of entering into any of those stories, perhaps if he ran into someone in a coffee shop, at a friend's house or in a hospital waiting room. What would he say, and how would he ever learn their story?

Jonah had extra time to consider the matter, and he recalled a lost opportunity one early morning about six months prior. He had an early breakfast meeting scheduled cross-town which involved a longer walk than the trek up to his office. Jonah decided to cut through Rockefeller Center. It was winter, the plaza ice rink was open and the Christmas tree was decorated. Jonah turned west off of Fifth Avenue on to 49th Street. In less than half a cross-town block he turned north through the plaza, the Christmas tree on one side and the skating rink on the other. It was too early in the morning for ice skaters, but too late in the morning for Christmas tree lights.

Jonah walked alone through the empty plaza surrounded by towering office buildings of art deco design. He came to a stop at 50th Street and waited for traffic to clear. Presently, two camels strolled up beside Jonah and looked down on him from a great height. This might have been an unusual sight except this was New York City where there is an explanation for everything.

The camels were on a leash. Jonah peered around the camels to see a young woman holding the leash. Jonah assumed camels needed walking, similar to some other pets. Surely, if anyone had a story worth probing, it had to be this woman. Unfortunately, Jonah was at a loss for a greeting appropriate for the occasion. All of his normal salutations seemed rather mundane for this exceptional encounter. The traffic was about to clear, so he had to think fast.

"Nice camels!" Jonah offered.

"Thanks," replied the woman as she walked away with her camels west on 50th Street.

If ever there was an opportunity to enter into a person's story, that had to be it. But Jonah blew it. Conversation is hard sometimes.

Jonah wondered where one keeps camels in New York City. He looked down the block and saw Radio City Music Hall at the corner. The annual Christmas show was in town.

CHAPTER EIGHT

JOY

Jonah stood in the morning sunrise studying ol' Lackawanna 1974, wondering what Greenwich looked like in 1974, who the commuters were and what they did. That was the year he graduated from college with great expectations but less wisdom. Jonah stood on the platform this day a much wiser man, but that gain was not without great loss, and great loss comes at a cost endured in a place of mourning. Maybe that is why someone once said: "All true wisdom is touched by sadness."[8]

Everyone will encounter sadness, but not all will mourn, because mourning is a voluntary response and a process. It must be chosen. Other choices are available, but they lead to dark places. We can choose bitterness, but bitterness is only a state of being with no clear way out. It is not a process with a beginning and an end, and a result which is better than the start. We avoid process because a process requires work. In this case, the work is the work of the second beatitude. "Without the work of mourning, the heart cannot move on from the thing that is lost to the thing that will replace it."[9]

Another response to sadness is to avoid pain by seeking happiness because it sometimes provides a degree of immediate relief. Happiness also involves work, but does not satisfy because it is a work-around, not a work-through. Therefore, ever increasing doses of happiness may be required to overcome the sadness. The result is exhaustion. To avoid pain is to avoid our humanity and to deny the process by which we are shaped. Life is difficult, so we will all experience difficulty or pain. The response should be a willingness to be shaped.

Someone once said, "we have to let go of what we want to get what we really need."[10] Maybe that was a loose paraphrase of King Solomon's words: "The heart of the wise is in the house of mourning,

---

8 Whitaker Chambers, *Witness*. (William F. Buckley, and Robert D. Novak). Washington: Regnery Publishing, 2005. (originally published in 1955).

9 Roger Scrutor

10 Michael Jr., in a spoken sermon.

but the heart of fools is in the house of mirth."[11] What we want is immediate relief or gratification. What we need is a refreshing result, and the second beatitude offers a refreshing result, which is that we will be blessed. That blessing looks like joy, the second fruit of the Spirit.

Jonah boarded the train considering the paradox that joy comes out of mourning. He decided to try this one out on Paul who was making his way down the aisle. Paul was always direct and to the point, because a conductor does not have time for long conversations.

"Paul, remember how I got stuck with the paradox of what being poor in Spirit has to do with love? Well, the second beatitude looks like another paradox. Does mourning lead to joy, or am I on the wrong track here."

"You're on the right track. Trust me. I'm the conductor."

Jonah told himself to be more careful with his metaphors.

Paul continued, "Think of what joy is about."

"What do you mean?" replied Jonah.

Paul continued, "People often use joy and happiness interchangeably. Maybe in this case they are not the same."

"Interesting you say that, Paul. Before boarding the train I had been thinking about mourning as a process instead of a condition. If so, then maybe joy is also not a condition, but a destination."

"And, maybe no matter how much you move in that direction, there is always more out in front of you," replied Paul. "That's especially true when it comes to mourning for sins, because there are always more of them. That kind of mourning is godly mourning, the kind when you really roll up your sleeves and go to work on a fresh start," he said as he moved toward the forward car.

Paul had a new thought, stopped, and turned around. "One more thing. Do not lose hope because godly mourning involves waiting. You're waiting for God to show up, and God does not disappoint." Paul walked back up the aisle and through the forward doors.

---

11 Ecclesiastes 7:4

Any mourning which involves waiting has to involve some serious introspection. That's when you go from mourning some sad circumstance to understanding your own contribution to the circumstance and taking ownership of it. Jonah had mourned the loss of almost everything, a wife, family, money, position and even health. He understood his part in causing that. Perhaps because of that recognition and a willingness to be reshaped, God was now restoring all things. God is a god of turnarounds, and recovering what was lost is a more gratifying experience than gaining for the first time.

Jonah also learned not to put his hope in circumstances. Another King Solomon saying came to mind: "When times are good, be happy; but when times are bad, consider this: God has made the one as well as the other. Therefore, no one can discover anything about their future."[12] Mourn in season, but don't lose your capacity for joy.

Jonah thought further about reconciling the apparent contradiction between mourning and joy. Maybe this was just one of those counter-intuitive things we just get used to accepting. There are fundamental contradictions in the natural world which are also hard to reconcile. What about the wave/particle duality of nature, or matter versus antimatter, or the Heisenberg uncertainty principal?

Jonah felt himself losing focus, but nobody wants to think about past misfortune, especially if it is rooted in neglect or bad behavior, like sin. Jonah could understand the usefulness of reflecting on behavior we can change, but what about mourning over things which aren't sins at all, just poor choices or unfortunate circumstances? Don't we all have regrets? Everyone regrets some things that are not overt sinful behavior, but which could have had a better outcome. Consider opportunities lost, the road not taken or the deed not done. Are we to mourn those things also? Regrets are not hidden from God any more than sins are. Jonah wondered what He would have to say about that, so he Googled "regret Bible." There appeared a potentially useful website called "Got Questions?" which suggested we acknowledge the unfortunate choice, event or outcome and ask God to use it for good, citing the sentence which says: "And we know that for those who love God all things work together for good, for those who are called according to his purpose."[13]

Jonah found another reference based on the Old Testament

12 Ecclesiastes 7:14 [NIV]

13 Romans 8:28

story of Lot's wife who turned into a pillar of salt when (contrary to an earlier instruction from an angel) she turned to look back at the destruction of Sodom from which she and her husband were escaping. The lesson was to avoid the appeal of the backward glance. Don't be like Lot's wife. She felt compelled to look back. One writer warns: "regret for what we have lost, for the pasts we have to abandon, often poisons any attempt to make a new life." [For those compelled to look] back at what has been rather than forward into the future, the great danger is [what] the Greeks knew was a narcotic pleasure, … a mournful contemplation so flawless, so crystalline, that it can, in the end, immobilize you."[14]

If mourning is a process it should not immobilize us. Mourning eventually gives way to joy because our God is a god of turnarounds. The greatest turnaround of all time was Jesus's death and resurrection. That was harder than any mourning we will have to do. But, what we can do is enter into the kind of "godly sorrow that brings repentance that leads to salvation and leaves no regret."[15] The effects of sin are not removed, but guilt is taken away. Guilt or regrets do not need to be carried forever like baggage.

Work would crowd out these thoughts, and Jonah would not revisit them for the remainder of the day. He had taken notes in a journal as was his custom, for truth is timeless. Even if these notes were not read again for days, months or even years, wisdom is too hard to come by to not record it.

It would not be reviewed further tonight. Jonah was tired from several meetings that day and was in bed by nine o'clock, even on a Friday. He entered a deep sleep, the kind which manufactures dreams. Dreams were nothing unusual for Jonah, but most fade quickly in the first waking seconds. Tonight's dream would linger in memory and take a special place in his journal.

Jonah dreamt he was sitting behind his desk at home. He heard a voice behind him. Though he could not see the speaker and there was no introduction, Jonah knew it was Jesus. Jesus said to Jonah, "Give me the file." Jonah did not speak but opened the desk's bottom right file drawer, leaned over and began lifting out a manila file folder marked "Sins." Jesus clarified, "Not that file, the Regrets file." The dream ended then without Jonah ever seeing Jesus, but he knew he

---

14 Daniel Mendelsohn, *A Search for Six of the Six Million*. Harper Collins, 2006.

15 2 Corinthians 7:10

had had a personal encounter with the ultimate source of all truth and wisdom.

CHAPTER NINE

PEACE

Jonah turned out of his driveway at the usual hour for the early train. Except this was Monday, so he would spend the first hour of his day meeting in an office near the Greenwich train station. The weekly Bible discussion group consisted of five to ten men, depending on who showed up.

The air was fresh and cool at 5:50 a.m. so Jonah drove with his window down. The sun was still low in the sky, but brilliant streaks of sunshine penetrated small spaces within the tree cover giving an almost kaleidoscopic effect from a moving car.

Jonah arrived in central Greenwich. He turned left and headed into the sun toward Starbucks. No 6:00 a.m. discussion was complete without that first, exquisite cup of black coffee. Even in June, Jonah preferred his coffee hot, the hotter the better.

Starbucks was the only coffee shop open before 6:00 a.m., so Jonah was grateful for the two men who staffed the store at this early hour. He imagined that anyone employed on this shift might consider it more than mere employment, perhaps a call to service or hospitality. Jonah recalled a recent book written by a former corporate middle manager who had lost his job in his 50's and had great difficulty finding comparable employment. Out of desperation the man took a Starbucks coffee shop job and was rewarded with a new sense of purpose when he realized he was in the business of providing immediate gratification and satisfaction to all who came to his counter, especially if each coffee was served with a smile. Jonah projected these happy thoughts onto the barista before him who presented him his very own black "grande" bold.

Walking back to his car, Jonah thought further about the former executive-turned-barista who asserted that the Starbucks job had "saved his life," figuratively speaking. The man had developed a new self which was neither executive, nor barista, but someone who belonged because he found meaning in serving.

Serving well requires humility, a trait essential for putting the needs of others above your own. Jonah thought about some of the people he admired most during his life, and they all had some degree of humility. It was never a conspicuous humility, but a humility which was always appropriate, gracious and never false.

Jonah thought about how humility emerges from the beatitudes. It seemed to relate to the third beatitude: "Blessed are the meek, for they shall inherit the earth." Jonah had always been uncomfortable with this expression because "meek" has become a tortured term with mostly negative connotations and therefore lost in common parlance. In the popular view, if the meek inherit the earth it has to be because everyone else has moved to a better neighborhood. The fictional Johnny Tremain was not insulted when Cilla gave a pious sigh and said: "When the meek inherit the earth I doubt Johnny gets as much as one divot of sod." Jonah determined to put the matter before the men's group as he pulled into the office building parking lot.

Jonah was the third person to arrive. Mitch owned the office, so he usually arrived first to open up. Woody had the furthest to drive, so he naturally arrived before those who had the shortest travel distances. Woody was more than a casual participant in this group. He was a PhD and a Pastor and therefore became the de facto oracle on abstruse matters ranging from original Hebrew and Greek manuscripts to scholarly exegeses and interpretations. He also had a clear eyed appreciation for how scriptures manifest themselves in lives well lived, born from his many years of missionary service in various world cultures. (Woody's office was less a place of business than a museum of African artifacts and memorabilia. Visitors to his conference table were always allowed the corner seat facing the center of the room to best appreciate the objets d'arts, which were plucked mostly from French speaking cultures and former colonies, for Woody was fluent in French.)

The train conductor's insights would be unavailable today, so Dr. Woody's would have to suffice. Group members were still arriving, so Jonah asked Woody about the third beatitude. He replied, "Meek is not the best translation, but it has becomes so ingrained into English translations that it is hard to shake. The dictionary has two definitions, and they imply very different things. One meaning seems to be the most common: submissive, or even timid. This is not at all the meaning in this context. The other use means patience combined with humility, which is much closer to describing the meek who will inherit the earth. The dictionary is right to associate meekness with patience, especially because real patience has no anger. We can endure injury without self-pity or a desire to retaliate because the Christian loves and knows how much he is forgiven. Only a very strong person can operate that way."

"So, this would be a kind of quiet strength," Mitch suggested.

"Yes, that would be a good way to think about it," Woody concurred. "There is nothing timid about quiet strength. Remember the passage that says: 'God did not give us a spirit of timidity, but a spirit of power, love and self-discipline.'[16] We expect to see power opposite timidity, but not love and self-discipline. This must mean that love and self-discipline are never part of timidity. On the contrary, love becomes a form of strength and self-discipline, and love from the self-disciplined person strengthens another."

By now, others had taken places around the conference table and were fully absorbed by the conversation.

Woody continued, "The dictionary also uses submission as a synonym for meek, but submission in a Christian sense involves relationships of love and respect. There is no timidity there.

"Biblical examples are sometimes instructive. Consider Moses who, according to scriptures, was the meekest in all the world.[17] He was also the greatest leader in the Old Testament, or perhaps of all time. Why was he great? Mainly, because he had God's power helping him. Meekness is the opening through which the Holy Spirit comes, to know what He knows, to hear what He hears, to speak as He would have you speak, to love as He loves. Humility is the appropriate posture for such a leader because it is the beginning of wisdom. All that would be reason enough to inherit the earth, and more."

Jonah replied, "Your comment about the posture of a leader is interesting. On a much smaller scale than the examples you gave, you may recall when I was called to become Senior Elder of our church board, one of the other Elders explained to me privately later: 'There was no one else. Humility comes before honor[18], and there is a lot of work to do.' The person was not looking to compliment me, because if I felt deserving or entitled I could not be humble, or meek. We are called to serve from a humble place where you don't think less of

16 2 Timothy 1:7

17 Numbers 12:3

18 Proverbs 15:33 and Proverbs 18:12

yourself, you don't think of yourself at all."[19]

Mitch interjected, "Isn't the phrase 'humility comes before honor' from Proverbs?"

"Yes," Woody replied. "In fact it is mentioned twice, which means it's important. For good reason. Humility is underneath all the fruit of the Spirit. And yet, as Chuck Colson said, 'humility is the most elusive of virtues because when you think you have it, you don't. Ironically, the more you have, the more you feel you need. That's because wisdom is not finite, and so God has to be the ultimate source of wisdom.'"

So, what is the connection between meekness in the beatitudes and its corresponding aspect in the fruit of the Spirit, peace? asked Jonah.

Woody replied, "Having a quiet strength frees a person to be more like himself, without pretentiousness. The root word of pretentious is pretend, and if you are pretending to be somebody else every day you can get pretty tired after a while. It is also hard to maintain that façade when things get difficult. The secret to being unpretentious is to trust in something other than yourself, so choose well. You can be more like yourself if you don't have to trust only in yourself.

Jonah replied, "Like Oscar Wilde said, 'Be yourself. Everyone else is taken.'" Jonah wasn't sure if that applied, but he could not resist.

"Peaceful means more than just being relaxed," continued Woody. "A man of peace must be a peacemaker. This is hard because a real peacemaker does more than suppress disagreement and discontent which continue to seethe below the surface of relationships. A true peacemaker resolves conflict. This requires strength, conviction, firmness of purpose and sometimes patience.

"A peacemaker needs patience because making genuine peace may involve a process. I love the story of Nehemiah who lived among the people of Israel during their exile as captives under Artaxerxes, king of Persia. The Israelites were a miserable, broken people. Nehemiah was a man of peace, but also a man of action who did not give up on his people.

"First, Nehemiah saw people who needed help, but he was

19 Chuck Davis

also patient. Before acting, he interceded for the people in prayer to God. Nehemiah was an assistant to the king and knew he was in a unique position to act. So he appealed to God for help: 'Give success to your servant today.' God opened a door. Once the door was opened, Nehemiah prayed once more. Finally, Nehemiah took hold of the authority God had given him and negotiated with the king for one of the great reconstruction projects of all time. The rebuilding of Jerusalem was one of the greatest peacemaking achievements in history for it resulted in the restoration of an entire people."

"Or consider the story of anxious Martha," said Woody. "She and her sister, Mary, once hosted Jesus for dinner at their house. Mary sat with Jesus to hear his teachings while Martha was distracted with much serving. Martha complained to Jesus that Mary left her to do the work, to which Jesus replied, 'Martha, Martha, you are anxious and troubled about many things, but one thing is necessary. Mary has chosen the good portion, which will not be taken away from her.'"[20]

"Sometimes when we choose the wrong things we become captive to our choices and they create anxiety without satisfaction. The point was not for Martha to relax, the point was to choose right – to choose Jesus."

20 Luke 10:38-42

CHAPTER TEN

PATIENCE

Jonah boarded the early train on Tuesday thinking about a dream he had the night before. In the dream he was a painter who admired the work of other artists and their ability to paint with various colors that Jonah could not replicate. Jonah could recognize yellow and admire its contribution in art, but he was unable to create it on his palette. So, he asked another artist where he could find yellow paint. The artist told Jonah to mix red and green. Jonah replied, "What is green?"

This was an odd story (particularly because Jonah was no artist), but odd in a way which begged for interpretation. Sometimes we know we are missing something we need. Perhaps we may have other areas of unknown or little understood need, and we lack the ability to recognize it. Jonah as artist realized he lacked yellow, but was blind to his lack of green. In the dream Jonah needed another person who knew about green to tell him he needed green.

Life is sometimes like that. We think we are complete people until somebody shows us otherwise, either by example or by speaking truth into our lives. Jonah wondered what color was missing from his palette which, he recalled, could have nine colors described as love, joy, peace, patience, kindness, goodness, faithfulness, gentleness and self-control.

Jonah thought about Ruth, who seemed to paint with all colors. Ruth rarely criticized Jonah if grace would suffice. He recalled a recent trip together in which a long drive was made longer by a tedious traffic jam. As the delay grew longer the car became quieter and Ruth could sense the tension in Jonah. Ruth broke the silence to say in a gentle voice, "It's alright, Jonah." That three-word sentence introduced patience where there had been none. Jonah always knew he was inclined to be impatient at times, but until Ruth's remark he never considered it a flaw to be addressed. Reflecting today on this incident, it occurred to him that a lack of one quality could be symptomatic of something else.

Jonah reflected on some occasions when he had been impatient.

Most times, impatience was stimulated by a desire to get something he wanted or to avoid something unpleasant. This desire could be a sign of selfishness or pride, especially if other people stand in the way of what we want. Even if we do not overtly conflict with others, a selfish impatience raises barriers between ourselves and others. Patience reduces barriers and turns a shared difficulty into a more pleasant relational experience.

Jonah figured he needed to add patience to his palette. How to do that? He remembered the parallel in the beatitudes: "Blessed are those who hunger and thirst for righteousness, for they shall be satisfied."

What is righteousness? Surely, it had something to do with doing the right thing, but there had to be a deeper meaning. Jonah was glad that for the price of the train ticket he could seek wisdom from his conductor, Paul, who was making his way into the car. "Paul," began Jonah as he flashed his monthly train pass, "What does righteousness mean to you?"

"Usually the only question I get at this hour," chuckled Paul, "is what time do we get into Grand Central? Let me see if I can shift gears. Righteousness starts with gratitude because it places the ultimate source of righteousness outside of yourself."

"What, then, after gratitude?" replied Jonah.

"God is always there to be grateful to, but there must be more to God than blessings or He would be just a one dimensional god. There is more about God to be experienced than blessing alone. God described Himself once as 'a God merciful and gracious, slow to anger, and abounding in steadfast love and faithfulness.'[21] We can't be these things all the time, so our righteousness is based on the extent to which we trust God to be these things."

Jonah replied, "Given all that, what does it mean to hunger and thirst for righteousness?"

"Hungering and thirsting for righteousness is much more than moving away from doing wrong. It involves moving toward something," offered Paul. "It changes your identity. And, it can be shared with others, which is how it operates as fruit of the Spirit."

---

21 Exodus 34:6

As Paul shuffled to the rear of the train car, Jonah reflected on how seeking righteousness relates to patience. The old saying, "patience is a virtue" was obviously true, but if it is the result of seeking righteousness then there must be much more to say about it. Jonah recalled Paul's notion of moving toward something. Indeed, hunger and thirst would propel a person strongly and urgently to overcome deficiencies of food and water. Any task of overcoming involves patience and, to continue the eating metaphor, "To him who overcomes, I will give the right to eat from the tree of life."[22]

Why doesn't everyone hunger and thirst for righteousness? Maybe because they think there will be no satisfaction at the other end. We tend not to trust the process. We tend to trust in ourselves. Self-reliance is a good thing if you really mean accountability. But everyone needs help sometimes. Trusting only in yourself wears you down. That is what God is for. He is not fickle, moody, capricious or conflicted in motives. He is someone you can trust. Trust in God gives a confidence which encourages patience.

Perhaps we don't trust the process because we don't trust the authority over that process. Maybe we think we know how life works, so we know what's best. But, there is a difference between knowing some things and knowing everything. The first step in admitting we don't know everything is to consider our sources of truth. Righteous people aren't righteous because they have all the truth. They are righteous because they are confident in their source of truth. The more we trust the source, the greater our understanding. It says "a patient man has great understanding,"[23] so I want to become a patient man.

Patience tests us during difficult times. Our first instinct is to escape the problem if possible. Some difficulties must be confronted. The mature person understands that problems and trials are part of life and we grow in the process. Jonah recalled an incident several years prior when he collapsed at work. An ambulance carried him to Cornell Medical Center in New York City where he presented with no discernible symptoms except a pulse of only 35, even in a fully waking and mobile state. Doctors determined to keep Jonah overnight for observation over Jonah's objections. He was moved to the cardiac ward.

A doctor and a team of interns visited Jonah's bedside and exchanged diagnoses, conversing among themselves as if he was not

22 Revelation 2:7

23 Proverbs 14:29

there. It appeared that they could not find anything specifically wrong with Jonah and, feeling better, he became impatient to leave the hospital. The doctors resisted and he resigned himself to a night in the ward. The room was surprisingly quiet considering the room housed eight patients. Most of them were too weak to make much noise.

The silence prompted a moment of reflection in Jonah, stimulated by the words "Be patient in affliction and faithful in prayer."[24] He realized his affliction (if indeed there was any) was trivial compared with the plight of his roommates. He felt slightly embarrassed by the contrast and determined to be patient in his comparatively small affliction. To whom, Jonah thought, should he be faithful in prayer? He looked around the room and the answer seemed obvious. Jonah left his bed and asked each patient in the ward, one at a time, if they would like prayer. Nobody turned him down, so Jonah prayed for each patient one-by-one. When he had finished praying in the ward, Jonah visited other rooms down the hall. He lost track how many heart patients he had prayed for that night. Jonah was blessed by a peaceful night's sleep.

The next morning, the hospital agreed to release Jonah, conditional on a routine doctor interview. This interview took place in the doctor's hospital office, not in the ward, and involved almost no medical questions over the course of fifty minutes.

24 Romans 12:12

CHAPTER ELEVEN

KINDNESS

Jonah rode the early train to the city thinking of the meeting he would chair that night. As Senior Elder of his church board he had been asked to address the group regarding the recent mission trip to Guatemala. Jonah had interpreted this trip as being a call on mercy, and he wondered how well he could bridge the space between the American rich and the Guatemalan poor. Even in his hometown, Jonah was either last among the rich or first among the poor, being neither heard by the rich nor known by the poor. He wondered if a condition of not quite belonging, yet not quite autonomous had bred in him kindness without empathy and generosity without compassion.

As the train pulled into the Grand Central tunnel, Jonah considered whether the fifth beatitude might inform his thinking about the evening talk. He recalled: "Blessed are the merciful, for they shall receive mercy." It fit well with its corresponding fruit of the Spirit, kindness. As the train rolled to a stop, Jonah recalled a dream in which he had died and arrived at the entrance to heaven where an angel guarded the gate. Jonah had brought a stack of folders with him which contained the entire history of his life. The angel asked him for the kindness folder. Jonah searched throughout the stack and found a single, thin folder labeled "kindness." Jonah opened the folder. It was empty.

Jonah reflected on his several encounters with one-leg John. He actually liked John, in spite of the language barrier. Therefore, Jonah was content to drop a modest sum into John's paper cup whenever he found him at the corner of 51st and Park. However, his morning train thoughts left Jonah with the uneasy feeling that he should be more generous to the one-legged man. Also, suppose he encountered another individual wanting help who seemed genuine, such as the "phantom" Asian man? Jonah separated the five-dollar bills from other currency in his wallet as charity reserved in advance.

Grand Central was positioned on the informal dividing line between the opulent business district on Park Avenue north and the lower rent offices and residences of Park Avenue south. Jonah's office was north, so he normally took the north end access, avoiding the terminal and emerging on 48th Street. But today, he walked through the terminal and out the main doors on 45th Street.

Jonah crossed 45th Street and walked through the Helmsley Building passage. He could see a woman with two children in a baby carriage on the next block. This was not the typical hour for strolling mothers. But, this was not a stroll. From a distance he noticed the woman trying unsuccessfully to capture the attention of the pedestrians in suits. As Jonah crossed 46th Street the woman approached him. Anticipating a monetary request, Jonah felt for the five-dollar bills he had stuffed into his right suit jacket pocket.

The woman was a surprisingly well groomed blonde, neatly but casually dressed with two children dressed with devoted parental care. As street panhandlers go, this family appeared abnormally prosperous. The mother approached Jonah, "Please, sir, would you help me?" She paused to see if Jonah would stop. He did. Jonah had a five at the ready for the expected request.

"Sir," the woman began, "could you please, please give me ninety five dollars."

Jonah was stunned. He let go of the five and let his hand fall limply out of his pocket. "Ninety five dollars! Ma'am, I don't have ninety five dollars!" Jonah exclaimed. Other pedestrians stared as they passed. Jonah returned to a quieter voice. "Why do you need ninety five dollars?"

"I have no home, the shelters are too dangerous for my family, and I know of a place I could stay the night on the west side for ninety five dollars."

"Ma'am, that's a lot of money to ask from a stranger on the street. Why did you think I could do that? asked Jonah.

"Because you were the only one who stopped," said the woman.

Jonah was not sure what to do, so he just walked away, feeling bewildered and a bit shaken. Soon, he was approaching 51st and Park and he could see one-leg John standing – always standing – facing north, holding his paper cup. At least Jonah knew what to expect from John, and called to him as he approached. John turned in an awkward hopping maneuver he had perfected with his crutches. John broke into a wide grin as if greeting an old friend. Jonah buried a crisp five in the paper cup.

In a stark departure from past practice, one-leg John withheld his normally profuse gratitude. Instead, he looked Jonah in the eye, and in the first full sentences he ever heard from John he said, "Do not give money every time. Just see me. Just say hi."

Jonah thought about the two personal exchanges he had in the very short distance between Grand Central and his office. Jonah occasionally gave to street beggars, the simplest of transactions in which few, if any, words are exchanged. Until today. Ironically, the first day ever in which Jonah tried to anticipate a need and came prepared to offer a larger sum was a day when the dollar amount was irrelevant and understanding was needed more. Perhaps God does not honor prepackaged charity. No amount is too little if offered with compassion. No amount is enough if offered without understanding.

The great advantage of missionaries over philanthropists is their personal understanding of the people they serve, their needs and what can best help those needs. The hard thing about being called to serve with money is that we feel the limits of our budget. If you serve with your heart you always have more to give.

Jesus twice quotes a scripture passage: "I desire mercy, not sacrifice"[25] where he rebukes an age old custom of sacrifice which had become corrupted into a short-cut to God's favor. Jonah considered the modern day equivalents of sacrifice.

Later that day on the train home, Jonah wrote some notes for his commentary to the Elders scheduled for that evening. He began:

> *As many of you know, I was raised in suburban Detroit and became an enthusiastic baseball fan from the moment I first set eyes on the beautifully manicured infield of Tiger Stadium. I even had a chance to sit in the press box for one game with the "Voice of the Tigers," Hall of Fame broadcaster, Ernie Harwell. Mr. Harwell was a kind man who would sometimes give kids a ride home from the ballpark. Decades later upon the occasion of Harwell's retirement he was interviewed on a sports program. The interviewer asked: "Ernie, you broadcasted baseball for sixty years. What single piece of wisdom would you like to share with our audience?" I thought he would say something like "good pitching beats good hitting every time," or "a five-man rotation is an improvement over a four-man rotation." Instead, Harwell quoted the Bible: "Act justly, love mercy, and walk humbly*

25 Hosea 6:6

with your God."[26]

If that was Harwell's best take-away after sixty years of broadcasting, I figured that might be wisdom worth thinking about. Since tonight's chat is supposed to be about mercy, consider the order of Harwell's citation. Justice and mercy are mentioned before walking with God, not after. First, our spirit and our sense of justice are developed, and then we are merciful. So, somewhere between our personal formation and seeing God comes a special way of relating to others through mercy.

Jonah considered his own experience. When blessings increase, the needs of others can't be far behind. Perhaps that is consistent with the Scripture verse: "Each one should use whatever gift he has received to serve others."[27] The gift is first received, and therefore not entirely yours to keep. Some people perceive their gifts as earned and hoard them. Other people see their gifts as undeserved and refuse them in their heart.

Jonah recalled a story of a pediatric cardiologist who performed surgery on a newborn baby with only two values in his heart. The normal number is four so the cardiologist installed two more valves. As the cardiologist explained to the parents, people need four valves, two to receive blood and two to dispense blood. There must be a balance between receiving and giving in every heart.[28]

People can lose the balance between giving and receiving. Society has assigned more of the duties of giving and receiving to government bodies which are just extensions of the law with no human capacity for mercy. Jesus said, "You…have neglected the weightier matters of the law: justice and mercy and faithfulness."[29] The law loses force and becomes corrupt without the moral foundation. Justice without mercy is tyranny. Mercy without justice is chaos. Mercy and justice are bound together by faithfulness.

Kindness is a fruit of the Spirit engendered by mercy. Sadly, society devalues mercy. Yet, mercy is essential for our personal development, for how can we be capable of reflection unless we are capable of mercy? They are both ways of stepping outside of ourselves.

---

26 Micah 6:8

27 1Peter 4:10

28 Analogy courtesy of Michael Jr., in a spoken sermon

29 Matthew 23:23

But these and other thoughts would have to wait for another time as there was too much to say and not enough meeting time to say it. The Elders would be waiting to approve the budget.

CHAPTER TWELVE

GOODNESS

Jonah overslept this morning so he was late to the train platform. The 6:37 express would be packed. Jonah looked down the long platform at a predominantly male crowd. More women take the 7:01 express train, and even more the later trains. Based on over thirty years of commuting, Jonah knew most of these men were traveling to Wall Street jobs. Several pulled wheeled overnight bags, indicating that they would head to the airport rather than home that evening. Their careers were stimulating and challenging, but much of Wall Street is a young man's business and Jonah (now over 50) was no longer a young man.

The young, affluent, upwardly mobile financier is a Greenwich caricature. The town is also home to a large group of middle class and working poor, primarily of Italian or African-American descent. While outward appearances of wealth may lead people to suspect a corresponding interior wealth, it is not the case. Our true wealth is our self-worth, measured by an inner character shaped by responses to life's events.

Our view of self becomes the currency by which we communicate with others. Some people feel rich in this currency, others poor. Some people think they are rich, and later find to their dismay they have been spending counterfeit money.

Jonah had once dreamed that he needed to scrape together some money. Starting with just a few coins in his pocket, he put the coins on a table. As he counted out the coins, they multiplied until there were too many to fit back into his pocket, and eventually too many to even count. Jonah reconsidered this dream as he boarded the 7:01 train. Ostensibly, a story of currency accumulation, perhaps it was a story about creation of inward identity, one coin at a time. Surely, this was a currency of value.

Goodness is a vague notion to most people, yet it is something almost everyone wants. If it is a vague thing, how do you develop it? Jonah recalled the counterpart to goodness in the beatitudes: "Blessed are the pure in heart for they shall see God." The pure in heart see clearly because God is the first thing they look for. They discern the difference between good and bad, between the good and the better, between doing what works for the moment and doing the best thing, the difference between the holy and the common[30], and the difference between what must change and what must not change.[31]

Strength goes with a pure heart. The great warrior, King David, said: "Create in me a pure heart, Oh God, and renew a steadfast spirit within me."[32] Strength is needed against the many forces that come against a pure heart. Some of these forces are external, like social forces. Others are internal, like discouragement or temptations. Physical strength requires courage at the testing point to reach its potential. Spiritual strength requires courage to reach its potential in a pure heart. Courage dissipates when we fear our highest possibility, evade the full intensity of life,[33] and give in to inferior values.

One inferior value is self-justification. We are so accustomed to justifying our behavior and even our thoughts that we often do not even know it is happening. We do this so that we can think of ourselves as good people. That is easier and less painful than the daunting task of exploring our own motives. We may not be as good as we think, even when we do good things, many of which come from mixed motives.

Jonah was as sure of these things as he was sure of anything, yet how did this enable him to "see God" as the beatitude says? It seemed like nonsense. Jesus assures us we will see Him in heaven, but the beatitude promises something here on earth. What does that look like?

Jonah was pretty sure we should not expect to see a physical Jesus in this world. Yet, he had heard the expression to "see God in everything" because this was His creation. But Jonah did not think he could appreciate the full dimension of that, no matter how pure in heart he might become. He also knew that we were promised the Holy Spirit, which is much more personal. It was not something he

---

30 Ezekiel 44:23

31 Rabbi Daniel Lapin, *Thou Shall Prosper: Ten Commandments for Making Money*. Hoboken, N.J: Wiley, 2013.

32 Psalm 51:10

33 Abraham Maslow, "The Jonah complex" is the fear of success or the fear of being one's best which prevents self-actualization or the actualization of one's own potential. It is the fear of one's own greatness, the evasion of one's destiny, or the avoidance of exercising one's talents.

would see, but upon reflection it occurred to Jonah that maybe "see" was needed as an impactful word for an ineffable and indescribable experience. "See" suggested something impactful and personal which words like "feel" or "experience" did not convey.

Jonah considered the possibility that he was not all that pure in heart, so perhaps he lacked the Holy Spirit. But, he recalled the remark, "It is possible to have some truth in the mind without Spirit in the heart, but never possible to have the Spirit apart from the truth."[34] Jonah had reckoned he had some truth so perhaps the Spirit was not far behind.

As God is seen to the pure in heart, so God is the source of all goodness – the sixth fruit of the Spirit. The attribute of being pure in heart and seeing God is an experience, unlike the first five beatitudes which describe ways of receiving something. Perhaps goodness also suggests a kind of God experience.

One manifestation of that experience is wisdom, for it says that "The starting point for acquiring wisdom is to be consumed with awe … of God."[35] Jonah's favorite definition of wisdom was: "Wisdom is the practical side of moral goodness."[36] So, wisdom flows from goodness, a godly attribute. If wisdom flows from goodness, which flows from God, then wisdom must conform to a certain natural order of things. Therefore, a life of goodness is a life which is most full when operating consistent with God's natural order.

The natural order is complex and often disturbed by misbehaving humans pursuing the worldly virtue of "freedom." Jonah marveled how the simple social notion of freedom became a human virtue, and an exalted one at that. Freedom has meaning in a social context, but is utterly meaningless as a defining description of the best life. Every life needs structure and direction to survive, grow and prosper. Goodness and its practical side – wisdom – offer a hope and a future, whereas freedom without wisdom leads nowhere except to confusion.

Jonah tried to record these thoughts in a journal that evening before retiring to bed. It was long and thoughtful work which can produce sleep through exhaustion. Tonight, it also produced a dream.

34 A.W. Tozer, *The Attributes of God: Based on The Knowledge of the Holy* [Harrisonburg, Va.]: [Christian Light Publications], 1990. (p.104)

35 Proverbs 9:10 (Passion Translation)

36 J.I. Packer, *Knowing God*. Downers Grove, Ill: InterVarsity Press, 2010. (p. 90)

Jonah saw himself at a banquet dinner seated at the end of a very long table which accommodated at least a dozen men, all of which sat along one side of the table facing out into the center of a room. Jonah was made aware that Jesus was also seated at the banquet, but at the very opposite end of the table. Jonah craned his neck to view Jesus, but could not see around the several men seated between them. Finally, Jesus leaned forward for the briefest of moments, but it was long enough for Jonah to catch a glimpse of Him. Jonah leaned back in his chair, satisfied. He had seen God.

CHAPTER THIRTEEN

FAITHFULNESS

Waiting for the early train in forced idleness is a good time to be alone with your thoughts. There are almost no people to talk to. The town is quiet at 6:00 a.m. Each day has its own opportunities and challenges, so each day needs new thinking. Much of life's excitement comes with the knowledge that yesterday's solutions may be of little help today.

Many of life's complexities do not lend themselves to formula solutions because they are fundamentally relational. The more people are involved, the more complex the challenge. We need wisdom to resolve these complexities. Jonah's analytical mind preferred to find a perfect solution by maximizing an objective function subject to constraints, but that method is often ill-suited for leadership roles. This morning, he pondered a leadership problem and hoped for wisdom.

Jonah was chairman of an organization which had economized on its proposed budget by eliminating a long standing financial commitment to another organization. The budget was approved unanimously by the board following the customary two preliminary drafts. Subsequently, Jonah received an objection from one board member who wanted to restore the excised budget item, and the person had been able to gather support to undo what had been passed.

Jonah thought this unfair to other constituencies which also experienced budget reductions. This presented a challenge in peacemaking. After careful consideration, Jonah decided to hold firm on the budget (for it had been fairly vetted and passed), but offered the board an opportunity to fund the special request out of their own pockets. He resolved to make his own contribution out of a spirit of constructive leadership. Peacemaking involves forming right relationships and the joining of people together. Jonah expected a good result because he believed these conditions already existed on the board.

Leadership is more about peacemaking than providing vision or giving direction. Beginning in humility creates an atmosphere for peacemaking later. Jonah remembered he was not chosen because he was great; he was chosen "because there was no one else." Therefore, a willingness to be led would be as important as the will to lead.

Why are peacemakers called "sons of God?" God always gets his way, but peacemakers often confront opposition. Jonah recalled that Jesus faced tremendous opposition from the political and social power structure of His day, and ultimately died from it. Yet, He never retreated into hate or vindictiveness, but sought reconciliation. Death on the cross was the ultimate form of reconciliation. You can't have true peace without justice, and justice always comes at a cost. Repentance by one party and forgiveness by another is one way of sharing cost which leads to a true and lasting peace. Forgiveness is not just a by-product of reconciliation. It allows it to happen.

If you are a son of God you might be a better peacemaker. Jonah considered some of the more difficult decisions he had to make in leadership. Sometimes he would pray for guidance, and sometimes he made decisions on the fly. He was unsure whether the former always turned out better than the latter. Any difficult decision is almost always opposed by some, so the question becomes one of how best to meet opposition. The best path is to draw on God's unlimited pool of wisdom. God's wisdom follows obedience and obedience follows faith, so true peacemaking requires faith. Leadership is more than a making correct decision or avoiding conflict; it includes strengthening of relationships.

As Jonah waited on the train platform for the early train, he wondered how peacemaking connected to faithfulness. He recalled one definition of faith: "being sure of what you hope for and certain of what you do not see."[37] We have faith in countless things, from the trivial to the momentous. Jonah had faith that the early train would show up (slightly less faith that it would show up on time). Consequences are small if that faith is misplaced, for he could always take the next train.

Suppose the early train did not arrive at all for two or three days running? Frustration would increase because Metro-North would be breaking faith with commuters. Some disgruntled customers would complain, but most would simply adjust their commuting habits.

Jonah considered faith invested in things of greater consequence. Suppose he calls "911" to report a burglary in progress in the home and the police do not show up. The stakes are higher, and the homeowner

37 Hebrews 11:1

is highly likely to complain to the police captain (assuming he lives to tell about it).

The police story may not create much of a public stir, being primarily of local interest. Jonah considered a matter of great consequence to many people, such as lax oversight of purity of a town's water supply. When this happened on an egregious scale in Flint, Michigan, town authorities were viewed as breaking faith, giving rise to organized political action at both the local and state level. Even Federal agencies were involved.

Breaking faith involves injustice because a mutual understanding has been broken by one party. Some cases are social injustices where the disadvantaged parties are a poor, weak or deprived group.

This thought provoked an interesting question for Jonah, which he expected could be answered momentarily, for the 6:07 train was pulling into Greenwich exactly on time. Paul could be counted on to be on time with both trains and answers. Jonah boarded through the rear doors and found his customary window seat in the emergency exit row.

Paul was already in the rear car, peering out the open window to check that all passengers had boarded. The train was soon on its way and Paul approached Jonah's row from behind. "Hey, man. Didn't see you yesterday. Oversleep or out of town?"

"The former," replied Jonah. "But I'm glad to see you this morning. Can I get some more free philosophy with the price of my train ticket? Is there a biblical connection between faithfulness and justice. I'm thinking that breaking faith is a breach of trust, which produces an unjust result requiring justice."

"Why are you asking?" inquired Paul.

"Because justice could be the link between faithfulness (the seventh fruit of the Spirit) and the seventh beatitude, peacemaking."

Paul enjoyed an intellectual challenge, so he did not mind delaying his routine to ponder Jonah's question. After a pensive pause, Paul replied, "You ask a deeper question than you know."

"How deep?"

"Deep as the very nature of God. What is God called?"

"Some say love."

"Who do you say that He is?"

Jonah was silent.

"You need a revelation. Try one. Look it up."

"Where?"

"Like I said, in Revelation. I'll be back."

As Paul walked away Jonah searched for what God was called in the book of Revelation. This was an odd book for its mystical visions and apocalyptic prophesies, so Jonah rarely ventured there. Those very qualities yielded up a stirring passage deserving of cinematic experience: "Then I saw heaven opened, and behold, a white horse! The one sitting on it is called Faithful and True, and in justice he judges and makes war."[38]

Paul returned on his rounds. "Did you find anything?" He asked.

Jonah read the passage from Revelation.

Paul reacted, "Love is not the only attribute of God. In fact, hundreds of years before that passage was written, another prophet wrote: 'The Lord is known by His justice.'[39] Or, as Tim Keller says, 'The Bible is a book devoted to justice in the world.'[40] Justice does not conflict with love; it is grounded in it. As it says: 'A throne will be established in steadfast love, and on it will sit in faithfulness…one who judges and seeks justice and is swift to do righteousness.'[41]

"There is your link between faithfulness and justice. Justice must follow faithfulness. But, this kind of justice -- the kind that follows faithfulness -- means more than bringing one party to account (judgment). It also means bringing one party their due (recompense)."

38 Revelation 19:11 (ESV, except the NIV uses "justice" in place of "righteousness")

39 Psalm 9:16

40 Tim Keller, *Generous Justice: How God's Grace Makes Us Just,* Penquin Books, 2012. (page xviii)

41 Isaiah 16:5

Jonah slowly absorbed Paul's last comment. The implications were far reaching. Justice in Flint, Michigan would mean more than bringing the municipal water company to account; it would mean ensuring clean water for town citizens.

The citizens' due is whatever justice requires. Justice comes at a real cost. People can't have justice without prior judgement, although modern society prefers not to judge. But, ideals are linked to judgments, so a society without judgments lacks substantive ideals. Without ideals we have an underdeveloped sense of justice which first tends to justify self, which leads to self-interest.

"Paul, I understand your points about justice, but how does that relate to peacemaking? Are they the same thing? Is peacemaking about fairness?"

"Even "fairness" is sometimes thinly veiled self-interest masquerading as justice," Paul replied. "Peacemaking is not necessarily just about fairness, especially in cases where a 'fair' solution is hard to determine. Overwrought fairness can crowd out generosity, yet sometimes the peacemaker's best solution is the most generous solution.

"God's works are always faithful and just,[42] but ours don't always work out that way in spite of trying. Human systems often produce unjust results. We can search for a better system, but even a better system will produce unjust results because it is still a human system. At what point do we stop looking for the best system and start applying Godly justice? Sin is not in money. It is in not caring. Caring and mercy involve self-sacrifice in a spirit of humility and faithfulness. Mercy undergirds justice."[43]

Paul paused, then changed the subject. "Jonah, my assignment on this train car has come to an end."

"I'm really sorry to hear than, Paul. I've enjoyed your company, but especially your wisdom."

Paul replied, "You already know the source of all wisdom, so you'll be fine."

---

42 Psalm 111:7

43 This is why Jesus said to the leader of the day, " . . . you neglect justice and the love of God." (Luke 11:42). Justice and the love of God belong together.

"I still have the last two beatitudes to go," said Jonah.

"I know. Don't worry. You'll get what you need," replied Paul as he turned and walked through the forward car door for the last time.

The train stopped at 125th Street and soon entered the Park Avenue tunnel. This was Jonah's cue to leave his seat and wait by the train door so he could exit before the crowd. He was soon joined by an unfamiliar conductor with a door key in hand.

Jonah offered up some conversation with the conductor. "Your partner, Paul, is a nice guy. Smart too. I'll miss seeing him on your crew."

"Who's Paul?", replied the conductor.

"You know, the conductor in charge of the rear cars on this train. He took over from Solomon about two weeks ago."

The conductor appeared baffled. "I've covered these cars myself since then. I don't know any Paul."

Jonah did not know how to respond. He would reflect often on the mysterious and wise Paul.

CHAPTER FOURTEEN

GENTLENESS

The sun rises early in June. This Tuesday morning was especially clear, brilliant and crisp as the sun rose across the pond. Jonah lounged comfortably on his deck with a black coffee in hand. Gratitude was in order and an entirely fitting mood for such a beautiful day. God's winning streak of 1.5 trillion consecutive sunrises was still intact, but today's had to be one of the best yet.

The sovereign force unfolding in nature also appeared to Jonah through the written word. Today's word challenged Jonah more than any of the previous seven beatitudes. "Blessed are those who are persecuted for righteousness' sake, for theirs is the kingdom of heaven." Nobody wants to be persecuted, so why allow yourself to be put in such a position?

Jonah could not recall ever being persecuted. He was grateful, for people are persecuted all over the world for the sake of greed, bigotry, power or other ignoble motives. Persecutors dishonor themselves by gratifying their own desires at other people's expense. By contrast, honor accrues to the person who is persecuted for righteousness' sake.

Ruth opened the screen door and stepped out onto the deck with her coffee. She chose the chair which would receive the first of the morning sun's rays. Ruth was as righteous a person as Jonah knew, so he posed a question to her.

"Ruth, I'm up to the eighth beatitude about persecution for righteousness' sake. There are lots of reasons in history for persecution (none of them good!), but I'm having a hard time understanding why anyone would be persecuted for righteousness' sake. Can you explain that?"

Ruth had the benefit of only a single sip of coffee and was still waking up. She took another sip to gather herself. "Christianity has always been countercultural, so authorities in power feel threatened."

"Christians aren't in it for political power," replied Jonah.

"Mostly true, but others don't know that. Christians do seek a following, and the secular world sees a following as the first step in seeking power and controlling the social order. Some regimes and authorities have no framework except self-interest for understanding a social movement."

Jonah replied, "Killing and displacing of Christians happens in many places today, but more subtle forms of persecuting Christians (like censorship) have emerged in western societies. That is harder to understand."

"Sad enough, but especially so for a society like ours which was founded on overtly Christian principles. In the U.S., Christians want the original norms back and appear reactionary to an increasingly secular society."

Jonah reflected on the implications of Ruth's remark. "This is more than just a difference of opinion. It's a conflict about which masters are to be served. For Christians, the answer is always God first. First before family, friends, country, everybody. For secular people, there must be some other ideal. I don't know what that might be, but freedom is often mentioned as the justification for almost anything. If freedom is the principle social ideal, then society might want to persecute Christians for freedom's sake; Christians would see themselves as being persecuted for righteousness' sake. The potential for conflict is obvious. Freedom to do anything you like is a self-centered argument. Righteousness is God-centered, by definition."

Ruth said, "Look at the bright side. We all have to go through difficult times and suffering. So, if you're prepared to suffer occasionally for your own sake, then why not suffer for righteousness' sake once in a while?"

"Maybe that's not much of a bright side, Ruth. Although that raises an interesting question. I might choose to live according to some of the other beatitudes, but I might not choose to be persecuted."

Ruth replied, "I'm not sure you ever choose that. You are led. You are led to it as a consequence of having lived the other beatitudes, because then you experience the fruit of the Spirit that goes along with each. You can't suffer anything (much less persecution) without some measure of love, joy, peace, patience, kindness, goodness and faithfulness. Besides, look at the bright side..."

"Uh oh, not the bright side again."

"If you are being persecuted for righteousness' sake, at least you know why you are suffering."

"I'm still not sure I would choose that," confessed Jonah.

"Understandable," replied Ruth. "But you might."

"Why?"

"First, because maybe you've realized freedom and happiness are not the same thing. Secondly, because Jesus never prayed to relieve Himself of inconvenience. If we open ourselves up to persecution for righteousness' sake, that is real purpose. The great thing about this beatitude is that it gives you the 'what' and the 'why'. I can think of other reasons."

"Such as?" asked Jonah.

"Persecution is what we endure, but it is not our problem to solve. Remember when (not yet king) David was in the wilderness because he was run out of town by Saul for no good reason? He complained bitterly to God, and God's retort was: 'Salvation belongs to the Lord.'"[44]

"And another reason?"

"Just as it says in the eighth beatitude, silly, 'for theirs is the kingdom of heaven.'"

"I guess that would be a big reward, alright."

"True. Bigger than even the Old Testament remedy."

"What remedy?" asked Jonah.

"The Old Testament proscribed all kinds of rules to live by, including rules of restitution. Sins of oppression were viewed as especially heinous, so the old 'eye-for-an-eye' formula did not work. Sins of oppression were penalized to the extent of 120% of the loss."[45]

44 Psalm 3:8

45 Leviticus 6:4-5

"So, if it is a good idea to endure persecution for the sake of righteousness, how do we do it?

"We need strength, especially against strong oppression. Paul of Tarsus was one of the most oppressed people in biblical history, so his example is a good one. He said: 'I have learned the secret of being content in any and every situation...I can do everything through Him who gives me strength.'"[46]

"I wonder how that works," asked Jonah.

"Perhaps through the eighth fruit of the Spirit – gentleness, which can also be called quietness. It says somewhere, 'The result of righteousness will be quietness and trust forever'.[47] It also says 'In quietness and trust shall be your strength.'[48] So maybe righteousness leads to strength through quietness (or gentleness). I don't think it is so much about being quiet as about what is going on inside you while you are quiet."

Jonah paused to let those thoughts sink in. "You might be right. If it starts with righteousness, then we need to be sure about what righteousness means. It is not a matter of simply doing a right thing. It is a matter of where your focus is. It is on Him who gives me strength.

"A lot of strength is needed if we are to respond to persecution with gentleness because persecution conflicts so strongly against our notions of fairness. Almost everyone eventually learns there is more to life than fairness; it's how you react when you are treated unfairly. And there is more to life than being right; it's how you react to being wronged. A Christian can understand that because it is the example that Jesus set. It is the example of goodness. The trap is thinking that it is enough just to be a good person without the Christ example, for that person is less equipped to respond well to unfairness."

Jonah considered the supreme example of unfairness in all of history, which is embodied in the ninth beatitude. But he put that thought aside as he was running behind schedule. It would be a slow day ahead, so Jonah did not mind taking a later train.

---

46 Philippians 4:12

47 Isaiah 32:17

48 Isaiah 30:15

CHAPTER FIFTEEN

SELF-CONTROL

One of Jonah's favorite ways to relax was with a cigar on the porch overlooking sunset. Ruth joined him on the deck, watching the birds around the pond. Jonah's cigar tasted even better at the end of a day. Anything seems possible during pleasant moments.

Possible indeed. Jonah recalled a solitary cigar moment filled with contentment, lacking only a friend with whom to share the occasion. Some experiences are just too exquisite to experience alone. Jonah's wish unconsciously drifted into a prayer, and in a brief moment an unfamiliar car turned into the driveway. It stopped alongside the porch, and Jonah's friend Dave surprisingly emerged from the car. Dave asked Jonah if he would excuse the unexpected drop-in, but said he could not resist showing off the smallest and most unusual of small cars. Swatch (best known for making watches) had apparently gone into the car business and Dave had become one of the first drivers of an oversized watch on four wheels. Jonah found another cigar for Dave, which was promptly lit to help celebrate this curious acquisition. What was lacking was supplied, and the evening was complete.

Jonah smiled as he recalled sharing a cigar moment with Dave. Dave could bring the unexpected, occasionally with some risk. He was fond of canoeing and Jonah had been included in multiple trips, always when the water was at its highest and fastest of the year. That was usually in late March or early April when weather was unpredictable. One trip started in a sleet storm, followed by ice floes competing with the canoes for space on the river. Jonah remembered the glazed look which comes over the eyes of a person experiencing hypothermia. Another trip unexpectedly involved a mid-river abandonment of canoes and a desperate swim for shore ahead of a class-five rapids which were, according to a popular river guide, "navigable only as a stunt."

Jonah asked himself why he repeatedly went along on Dave's risky rides. Adventure had its allure, but only up to a limit. Beyond that limit, trust has to take over. Jonah trusted in Dave's good judgement based on prior experience on these same rivers and others like them. He also trusted in the maritime experience of his Navy SEAL son who ably captained their canoe from the rear seat. (Jonah did not expect a need to trust in his son's swimming experience in rough waters, but that trust also turned out to be well placed.)

Trust is useful on an unfamiliar river, but indispensable for understanding the ninth beatitude: "Blessed are you when others revile you and persecute you and utter all kinds of evil against you falsely on My account. Rejoice and be glad, for your reward is great in heaven…." How can anyone be expected to rejoice and be glad for being reviled, persecuted and receive evil utterances, all for the sake of an unimaginably speculative promise in the distant future? This future hope requires extreme trust, even greater than the trust needed to navigate extreme rapids or ice rivers.

Is such trust possible? Jonah was unwilling to die on the river, but Jesus was willing to die on the cross. And, that was after he was reviled, persecuted and received evil utterances. Christ modeled exemplary trust. We all trust someone, but as the stakes get higher we won't trust just anyone. When we play for the ultimate stakes, we trust the One who is true, for true is the root word of trust.

Trust is more than loyalty. The disciple Thomas spoke out of loyalty at Lazarus' death when he said, "Let us go, that we may die with him." But Thomas' trust fell short when he confronted Jesus after His resurrection saying, "Unless I see the nail marks in His hands…I will not believe it." Thomas then learned that trust in the Son of God involves trust at a whole other level. God is faithful to this trust. "The one who trusts in Him will never be put to shame."[49]

We can trust an authority if we believe in the truth for which it stands. The greater the truth, the more we can trust to the point of great sacrifice. Trust in the highest ideal is completely selfless, so sacrifice is made even without expectation of benefit. Jesus commands the highest trust because He embodies the ultimate truth.

Jonah wondered how people live under the popular notion that "there are many truths." Are these "many truths" all equally valid and equally important? If so, what happens if they conflict which each other? If not, what measure of devotion does one give to one versus another? Under what truth would an authority rule, and could that authority expect an equal measure of devotion from all those under authority? What would a person sacrifice for the sake of "many truths?" These are not theoretical questions. They affect how we operate in our

49 Romans 9:33

daily lives.

If duty is required, we want to know the authority which asks it. When John F. Kennedy said: "Ask not what your country can do for you; ask what you can do for your county," listeners had a generally shared understanding of the authority which called citizens for duty. What an even greater calling to declare, "I want to know Christ and the power of His resurrection and the fellowship of sharing in His sufferings."[50] The first part sounds appealing, the second part repelling. The harder a duty, the more trust must be vested in an authority.

Jesus came to give us more than information. He gave us a covenant relationship worthy of trust. Any great trust involves duty, but if we are to concede duty it must be to a trustworthy authority, not to an untrustworthy power, for authority ultimately trumps power.[51]

A call to duty requires trust, so a call to the highest duty requires faith. A person of faith has self-control, the ninth fruit of the Spirit. Without self-control we cannot with grace experience, endure, persist and ultimately prevail over pain or great difficulty. Jonah did not always trust his self-control because he knew himself to be an impatient man. He wondered if he lacked self-control in ordinary matters, how would he do if others "reviled, persecuted and uttered all kinds of evil against him falsely" on Jesus' account. How much self-control would he have then? Self-control has to come from faith when the stakes are really high: "The goal of faith is the salvation of our souls."[52]

Jonah concluded he was still a work in process. Duty requires trust, but also a willingness to suppress his own needs and desires for the sake of something greater. Jonah knew that fear could interfere with that, but he did not consider himself a fearful person. Pride could also get in the way because pride is a way of elevating ourselves above others. Jonah saw this flaw in himself even though he could identify no logical source of pride. He was not extremely wealthy, not at all famous, and certainly not the best looking. Perhaps there is a human tendency to create images of ourselves which are not real. Jonah concluded that pride undermined his self-control because it blocked humility. Without humility there was no one to trust but himself.

Jonah remarked to Ruth, "I'm thinking of the ninth and last beatitude, the one about enduring persecution for Jesus' sake. I figure

50 Philippians 3:10

51 Chuck Davis, in a spoken sermon.

52 1Peter 1:9

it's a lot about trust. Trust is about what we believe, but we do not always act according to what we believe."

"Let's pick an example," suggested Ruth. "Consider the disciple Peter. Famously, he chickened out and disclaimed Jesus three times, and this after he had spent three years with Jesus and acknowledged Him as the Son of God. I'm guessing he trusted Jesus, so there has to be another explanation. Simply, Peter was just human, and he was just afraid."

"Makes sense to me," replied Jonah. "What's interesting is that when Jesus next saw Peter after the resurrection He did not tell Peter he failed the ninth beatitude and too bad for his chances in the kingdom of heaven! Instead, Peter was reinstated."

"Thankfully, it's not about being perfect," added Ruth.

"It makes me wonder what Jesus was promising when he said '… your reward is great in heaven, or …theirs is the kingdom of heaven,' replied Jonah"

"I don't remember Jesus ever describing what heaven looks like. The beatitudes characterize it by how we will be and who we will be. We will be righteous. As you know, this does not mean perfect. It means putting God first. Jesus calls heaven a kingdom, which means there is a King. This makes a good metaphor if we are putting God first. Kings are considered first in their kingdoms. Presidents are only, well, fancy executives," Ruth added with a grin.

"You're right, Ruth. I can think of no passage which describes heaven's geography or what it looks like, though I am sure someone must have asked Him. (Maybe that is for someone who is still thinking about whether he wants to go there.) Jesus doesn't refer to it as a *place*, anyway. He just says it is 'theirs'."

"And, He always uses the present tense: 'theirs is,' not theirs will be," replied Ruth. "Sounds like a guarantee. And a guarantee is unconditional. If it's unconditional, we don't have to be perfect."

Ruth and Jonah fell silent as a belted kingfisher circled the pond, spotted his prey just beneath the surface and hurtled toward the water below.

CHAPTER SIXTEEN

LOGIC

The sun rose early Saturday morning over the pond. The June morning sun shines directly onto the deck, unlike the colder months when the light angles from a more southerly direction and is blocked by tall Adirondack trees. These were mornings to savor. No activity was apparent in the other homes surrounding the pond. Jonah's coffee was welcome company.

Such moments are made for the mind to wander, but Jonah's thoughts turned to his business. Revenues had increased more than expected, and a large firm had bought him out. Jonah still managed the business as before, so financial reward did not translate into complacency. As any participant in the capital markets knows, something new is always about to happen, perhaps something utterly unanticipated. So the mind is always unsettled, looking for the fatal flaw in the structures people have created.

Investment banking had been good experience in discerning business flaws in corporate strategies and operations. Jonah had many conversations with chief executive officers, chief financial officers and others, and he was struck how differently skilled they were, even within the same industry. Those differences often seemed to explain relative profitability. This perspective was illuminating for understanding management flaws, but cautionary for an overconfident analyst and reminiscent of the laughable parable of the man with a "plank" in his eye criticizing the man with a "speck" in his eye. The fatal flaw may be closer than we think.

Notwithstanding this caution, we still search for the most workable formula. Jonah once thought he had one. Informed by his investment banking experiences, he had developed a model indicating some predictive power in a long/short investment strategy in utility and power equities. Preliminary results were so encouraging that he and a partner were hired by a $3 billion private hedge fund to implement the strategy. The model worked for a time until results flat lined. Jonah was suddenly out of the hedge fund business. Jonah concluded that there was no enduring magic investing formula.

Life in general defies formulas. There is a saying: "man plans and God laughs." God does not really think it is funny when we struggle or encounter tragedy. He wants to help, even if that help comes only in the form of endurance and strength. The truth underlying the quip is that life is full of unpredictable variables and complexities. As all married couples know, even the interactions of just two people can become difficult. Imagine how much more difficult is a life which intersects with thousands of individuals over a lifetime!

We desire formulas because we desire a rational world. But human rationality is only a matter of making finer calculations which can never satisfy human desire for a just, moral and loving culture. It has been said: "Sure, there is a logic to the mind. But, the soul has a logic that might be more compelling than the mind's.[53] We make rules and laws to provide a livable order. However, "Rules will never give us answers to deep questions of the heart, and they will never love you."[54]

We cannot rely on formulas or rules to avoid difficulty, so we need to know what to do when life just is not working. The beatitudes are not a formula, but they are a foundation for a life well lived in community. They are a process, not an end result. As in any process, we must sometimes wait so things can come in the proper order. We also wait to renew our strength,[55] because the construction of anything worthwhile involves hard, tiring work. Waiting also provides confidence that the end product will be worthy and fully formed: "Those who wait for Me will not be put to shame."[56]

We will not wait unless we believe in the process. "Whoever believes will not be in haste."[57] If we believe in this particular process, we know how to wait, which is in prayer. If we are in prayer, we also know when we are not following the process. Knowing when to wait and how to wait makes the process fruitful. The work of this process conditions our spirit, but the Spirit is something we are given. We do not earn it.

---

53 Whittaker Chambers, *Witness.* (William F. Buckley, and Robert D. Novak) Witness. Washington: Regnery Publishing, 2005. (originally published in 1955) p.14.

54 William P. Young, *The Shack: Where Tragedy Confronts Eternity.* Windblown Media, 2007.

55 Isaiah 40:31

56 Isaiah 49:23

57 Isaiah 28:16

The Spirit speaks through the beatitudes, the best formula, for the beatitudes are flawlessly formed, logically coherent, symmetrically designed and elegantly inductive. The logical progression begins with four beatitudes which relate to the development of self. The fifth beatitude addresses our relationships with others. The last four speak to a person's relationship with God. The second stage builds on the first, and the third stage builds on the second in a symmetrical 4-1-4 balance.

The beatitudes also display a symmetry of fours. Each of the first four beatitudes corresponds to a related beatitude in the second group of four. We see each of the first four beatitudes as a characteristic needed for the emergence of the corresponding characteristic in the second four beatitudes. Thus, the first beatitude (in which being poor in spirit becomes the condition for the ability to love) enables us to become merciful and kind to others. The second beatitude (in which mourning cleanses the heart) prepares a person to be pure in heart as described in the sixth beatitude. The third beatitude describing Jesus' quiet strength enables us to be the peacemakers described in the seventh beatitude. Finally, the fourth beatitude calling for righteousness provides the ability to be persecuted for righteousness' sake in the eighth beatitude. One final symmetry is shared by the first and eighth beatitudes, which both guarantee that "theirs is the kingdom of heaven."

The beatitudes operate as an integrated whole. They are not selections on a menu in which more of one compensates for lack of another. They feed us fully only when taken together because the beatitudes are the path to character formation.

Character emerges in the fruit of the Spirit: love, joy, peace, patience, kindness, goodness, faithfulness, gentleness and self-control. Some consider the fruit of the Spirit as a few of several aspects of good character, suggesting several other qualities which could just as easily have been included. However, if we consider these nine qualities as closely connected to the beatitudes, then they take on a significance above others.

Other exemplary qualities are so closely linked to one of the fruit of the Spirit as to be comprehended by it. So, for example, generosity might flow from kindness and unselfishness from love. What about the much proclaimed and honored virtue of courage? "Courage is not simply one of the virtues but the form of *every* virtue at the testing point."[58] All of the characteristics described by the fruit of the Spirit may require courage to reach their fulfillment in times of crisis or high stress, but they are not themselves courage.

Whatever has happened to you is less important than how you were changed. We can resist change, we can manage our own change, or we can cooperate with the Holy Spirit in our own character formation. Your choice. "How you handle your present depends on what you perceive your future hope to be."[59] Is your hope in a better reputation or in a better character? "Reputation is what people think you are; character is what God knows you are."[60] Is your hope in better comfort or in better character? God cares more about your character than your comfort."[61] The better hope looks beyond just the next day. The best hope extends from everlasting to everlasting.

The impersonal society struggles because it has placed its hope in rules but has overlooked the value of character. The impersonal society believes nothing because it has no theory of character formation, save for a codification of "do nots." What are the consequences for character? "We make men without chests and expect from them virtue and enterprise. We laugh at honor and are shocked to find traitors in our midst."[62] Society has bred men and women without courage and incapable of encouraging others.

A land without character is a land without community, for nothing of enduring worth is shared. The less is shared, the more we hoard and the land becomes arid and lifeless. But the fruit of the Spirit grows even in a desolate field because it is meant to be shared, and the streams that water it never run dry.

The fruit of the Spirit is the work of the Spirit in us. That involves work for us because character comes at a cost.[63] There are no shortcuts, but the destination is worth it. Jonah recalled a dream in which he walked along a road with a long procession of people. Most eventually came to a standstill, but Jonah and a few others kept walking. As Jonah turned to look at the stragglers a voice came saying, "Don't look back.

---

58 C.S. Lewis, *The Screwtape Letters.* New York: HarperCollins, 1942. (italics added)

59 Tim Keller, spoken sermon on Revelation 21.

60 Martin Sanders, discussion comment

61 Chuck Davis, from a spoken sermon.

62 C.S. Lewis, *The Abolition of Man.* New York: HarperCollins, 1943.

63 Howard Chickering

You are going to meet Jesus."

CONCLUSION

Events shape us. Sometimes even a small forgettable event impacts us in unexpected ways. Consider a word from a friend, a simple kindness, or even a chance encounter with a stranger. If we are not alert, in too much of a hurry, or preoccupied by the day's busyness, the incidentals of life fly past our consciousness and are lost forever.

I never realized how many simple yet meaningful experiences filled my life until I kept a journal. Your life is a rich accumulation of events and reflections. Don't lose them. Write them down.

ACKNOWLEDGEMENTS

Experience is a great teacher, but not the only teacher. Much wisdom is close at hand through the counsel and perspective of others, whether scholars, professionals, co-workers, or just friends. All have filtered wisdom out of their own unique experiences and learnings.

This manuscript reflects much such wisdom collected from friends, casual acquaintances and even chance encounters too many to name. Where memory is clear and specificity is possible, footnotes give credit, for some narrative would have been lifeless without them.

An author's job is to weave many thoughts into a coherent whole. My advisor and friend, Bob Trexler, was more than my editor, for his skill in straining the wisdom out of the words supplied much of what was first lacking. This book would not have been possible without him and his always thoughtful contributions and patience.

Two friends deserve special credit for wading through the thicket of an early draft. Pastor Joan Osgood kindly vetted the theological content to keep me from committing any heresies. Maria Mata's credentials as a professional educator remain intact thanks to her able proofreading and teacher's eye for misspellings, misstatements and misplaced verbs.

My wife, Maria, deserves credit as a reader of drafts, but much more as a real life participant in this story. The representation of her in this *roman à clef* is but a poor reflection of the real-life joy and faith embodied in her.

Memories fade, so important credits may be lost to time. Credit is due nonetheless to those who contributed without knowing. Any errors in recollecting or in telling remain mine.

www.ingramcontent.com/pod-product-compliance
Lightning Source LLC
LaVergne TN
LVHW051016080826
845145LV00009B/2645

* 9 7 8 1 9 3 5 6 8 8 3 1 0 *